Until June

Barbara M. Britton

D1202594

This is a work of fiction. Names, characters, places, and incidents either are the product of the author's imagination or are used fictitiously, and any resemblance to actual persons living or dead, business establishments, events, or locales, is entirely coincidental.

Until June
COPYRIGHT 2020 by Barbara M. Britton

All rights reserved. No part of this book may be used or reproduced in any manner whatsoever without written permission of the author or Pelican Ventures, LLC except in the case of brief quotations embodied in critical articles or reviews. eBook editions are licensed for your personal enjoyment only. eBooks may not be re-sold, copied or given to other people. If you would like to share an eBook edition, please purchase an additional copy for each person you share it with. Contact Information: titleadmin@pelicanbookgroup.com

All scripture quotations, unless otherwise indicated, are taken from the Holy Bible, New International Version(R), NIV(R), Copyright 1973, 1978, 1984, 2011 by Biblica, Inc.™ Used by permission of Zondervan. All rights reserved worldwide. www.zondervan.com

Scripture quotations, marked KJV are taken from the King James translation, public domain. Scripture quotations marked DR, are taken from the Douay Rheims translation, public domain.

Scripture texts marked NAB are taken from the *New American Bible, revised edition* Copyright 2010, 1991, 1986, 1970 Confraternity of Christian Doctrine, Washington, D.C. and are used by permission of the copyright owner. All Rights Reserved. No part of the New American Bible may be reproduced in any form without permission in writing from the copyright owner.

Cover Art by *Nicola Martinez*
Prism is a division of Pelican Ventures, LLC
www.pelicanbookgroup.com PO Box 1738 *Aztec, NM * 87410
The Triangle Prism logo is a trademark of Pelican Ventures, LLC
Publishing History
Prism Edition, 2020
Paperback Edition ISBN 978-1-5223-0289-6
Electronic Edition ISBN 978-1-5223-0288-9
Published in the United States of America

Dedication

This book is dedicated to the men and women of the United States military, past, present, and future, who faithfully serve our country. Thank you for your sacrifice and service.

1

Juneau, Alaska, September 1918

Josephine Nimetz slipped into a perfect replica of a wool coat, one she had drawn, designed, and patterned on old newspaper. She tucked a rectangular box under her arm and tiptoed across the living room toward her mother who slept in an oversized chair. Laying a gentle hand on her mother's swollen knuckles, she whispered, "I'm off to the Chambers Estate."

Her mother's eyes fluttered open. "I thought you delivered Mrs. Chambers's gown yesterday?"

"Yes, but Ann forgot to put the gloves and embroidered handkerchief in the box. I don't want any complaints from our best customer."

"Your sister can't seem to think about anything these days. Anything, that is, except men."

Josephine stepped toward the door. At seventeen, the last thing she wanted to discuss was her sister's courtships. There had been too many stories of lonely miners with gold rush dreams.

Her mother coughed and leaned forward.

Josephine halted. "Do you need your medicine?"

"At night dear. Only at night." Her mom sat back

and closed her eyes.

Clenching her teeth, Josephine crossed over the woven rug and rested a hand on her mother's forehead. No one should suffer in order to save money. "I'll steep us some tea when I return." She stroked her mother's hand.

Using Mrs. Chambers's package to shield her cheeks from the salty sting of brisk Alaskan air, Josephine scuffed along the walkway bordering tiny, wooden row houses. The homes, nestled on the side of a mountain, were one earth-shattering jolt away from plunging into the Gastineau Channel.

She stopped briefly in town to inspect the fashion ensemble in the department store window. The same dusty, shipped-in gown from the previous month clung to the dressmaker's dummy. Good. No new arrivals to compete with this week.

Trudging past the stained glass Russian Orthodox Church and up the hill toward Juneau's elaborate homes, she spied the Chamberses' mansion with its gabled roof and large bay windows. One day, she hoped to own a big home with a formal dining room and a sizeable porch; a place where her mother could survey comings and goings from outside the front door—rain or drizzle. "Someday," she sighed. Definitely, not now.

As she neared the Chamberses' gardens, a man staggered in her direction. His limbs flailed like a drifter kicked out of the Red Dog Saloon at closing time. A cap shaded his face except for his days-old beard, but she knew that uneven gait. Ivan? Couldn't be? Her stepfather worked on Douglas Island—at the mine. Lately, on days off, he stayed on the island with his paycheck.

"It's about time."

Josephine's pulse quickened. She recognized her stepfather's sharp sarcasm.

Ivan's calloused hand engulfed her shoulder as the stench of Skagg whiskey accosted her nostrils.

"Where's the money?" His words slurred together.

"What money?" She cradled Mrs. Chambers's box against her chest, grateful for the distance it put between them.

Seizing her collar, Ivan curled the fabric into his fist. "Mrs. Chambers pays you fourteen dollars for those fancy dresses." His grip tightened. "You'll give me the money."

"It's gloves." She fumbled to open the top of the package. "I don't have any money."

Scarlet capillaries streaked her stepfather's bulging eyes. "I need it."

Words stuck like cotton in Josephine's throat. "But…but your pay from the mine? You got paid?"

He lifted her lapel closer to his face. His sour breath tainted the air. "Don't hold out on me, girl. That pay's gone."

What of mother's medicine? Heat flushed her cheeks. She dropped Mrs. Chambers's accessories and clawed at his forearm, easing the pressure on her neck.

"Look for yourself. There's no dress. That money paid off our credit at the store." She avoided Ivan's hazel-eyed glare.

"That's not your place, girl."

Sing-song laughter sliced through the pine trees.

Mrs. Chambers. Thank God. Josephine strained to see her customer.

Ivan cursed and released her collar. His ragged fingernails gouged her neck. A burn like booted-up campfire embers sizzled along her throat. He bent to pick up the box. The crushed corner revealed embroidered cotton.

"These worth something?"

"No. Not to you." Her words came out in an almost-shout. She lunged to collect her work.

"Josephine?" Mrs. Chambers's inquiry held a hint of concern.

Ivan pushed off to flee. His stiff-armed thrust sent Josephine tumbling backward. Her head struck something hard. Searing pain sliced into her scalp while vibrant bursts of light blurred her vision. A glacier-ice chill crept over her flesh. *I need to get up and deliver the gloves. Mother needs her tea.*

When she opened her eyes, darkness greeted her. Instead of the hard ground, silk sheets caressed her skin and mounds of soft pillows buffered the pounding rhythm in her forehead. Moonlight peeked under tall curtains and revealed the outline of claw-footed furniture. The scent of Mrs. Chambers's rosebud and lily perfume hung in the air. How had she gotten inside the Chamberses' house?

A deep undulating moaning crept into the bedroom, followed by a panicked scream.

Josephine sprang upright. Her head spun, the room spun, everything spun. She massaged her throbbing temples. Did her mother know where she was and what Ivan had done?

A man's cries filled the hallway. The hair on her arms rose to attention like fur on a hissing cat.

She wrapped a pillow around her head to drown out the moaning. Linen grazed her neck. What happened to her long locks? Reaching back, her fingers discovered chopped-off hair and a stitched bump covered with greasy ointment. The mat in her hair was round like a bird's nest. A cap would be in order to cover this mess.

Rolling to the side of the bed, she slowly stood. Pain ricocheted through her face. She braced herself with a hand on the nightstand and fumbled her way to the door, trying not to trip on the length of her borrowed night dress. Someone had changed her. She stiffened. She needed to find out whom. She needed to find out what had happened. She needed to find out if Ivan had bothered her mother.

As she opened the door, light from engraved sconces in the hallway illuminated her room. Crystal glasses glimmered on the nightstand. A small R, larger C, and a small J were embossed on the matching pitcher. She ran her fingertips over the grooved letters. Reynold James Chambers. He owned land, lumber mills, and gold mines, and his wife paid top dollar for one-of-a-kind gowns. Even the bows on Josephine's night dress were a special order.

"Water," a voice pleaded. "Some water."

She held her breath and listened.

The pitiful sobbing from down the hallway made her injury seem insignificant.

Was Mr. Chambers ill? His son had recently returned from the war. Perhaps he or a servant suffered. Certainly, someone would comfort the man.

The crying stopped. Raspy shouting for a drink took its place.

Curious about what was going on, Josephine peeked down the hallway. A woman paced, head down, hands folded, outside a door at the other end of the hall. Her measured steps were precise as a wind-up toy. It looked like Mrs. Prescott, the Chamberses' housekeeper. After a couple of laps, Mrs. Prescott scurried off. The maid's footsteps clamored on the stairs.

Josephine turned and stared at the pitcher of water by her bed. The Chambers had taken care of her injury. Returning a favor was customary. After all, Father Demetriev had preached, 'do unto others' at mass.

She poured a glass of water and swerved down the hallway, steadying herself with a hand to the wall, and careful not to spill on the plush rug. She stood in front of the door. Muffled sobs came from inside. Her heart plummeted to her belly. Her mother cried like this when her joints flared with pain. Sucking in a deep breath, she knocked softly and ducked into the unknown.

An eerie lemon-yellow glow came from a lamp on a nightstand. A man, younger than Mr. Chambers, lay in bed with a blanket covering the bottom half of his body. His nightshirt clung to his chest, wet with perspiration. A faint odor of rubbing alcohol and urine filled her nostrils as she entered the bedroom. She breathed through her mouth to calm her stomach.

The man turned his head to gawk at her as if she had materialized from a puff of magician's smoke. He stared with sunken gray eyes, underscored by purple half-moons. Brown hair hung over his ears, sticking to the side of his face, framing the stubble of a beard. Josephine steadied the glass in her hand. The man looked her sister's age—not more than twenty—but frail for his youth. If this was Mr. Chambers's son, he didn't resemble the young man she had seen driving a Model-T around town. With all the deliveries she had made to the Chambers Estate, she had only glimpsed Geoff Chambers once. Even then, he was scurrying out the door to some urgent event.

She held out the glass and moved closer to the bed, ready to run at the slightest hint of danger.

The man studied her approach. He lifted his hand to take the water glass but never shifted his focus from her face. He drank the water in one gulp.

"What's the matter?" she whispered.

"Only that everyone seems to have gone deaf." He handed her the glass. "What's wrong with your hair?"

"I injured my head." She fingered her scalp. "I guess I'm lucky it didn't kill me."

"You're not dead," he said, straightening the bed sheet. "I should be."

Her mouth gaped as if she was eating a fork full of greens. Was he serious?

He sank back onto his pillow. "Refill that for me. I'm awfully dry."

Josephine nodded. Once.

Slipping back to her room, she filled the glass and glanced down the hall for Mrs. Prescott. Thankfully, the floor didn't buckle in her vision and cause her to swoon.

She headed toward the sick man's room and opened the door without a knock. Why wake her hosts? The man knew she was coming. Hurrying toward the bed, she reached out her hand.

He went to seize the glass. Stepping forward, her foot caught the edge of a throw rug. She catapulted forward. Before she could steady herself, water cascaded over the man's chest.

Gasping, he shot up into a sitting position. Liquid soaked into his shirt, dripping onto the sheet below.

He cursed.

Josephine blinked her eyes rapidly as if she was

watching a black and white Flicker Film. "I'm so sorry."

"It's all right." He held the shirt away from his skin. "I've had worse."

"Let me help." Grabbing a cloth from the table, she blotted his nightshirt. Her fingers slid down over his thigh and then bent sideways over a ledge of flesh. Her hand descended like an anchor toward the mattress. No muscle or bone buoyed her weight. In steadying herself, she pressed on his other thigh.

His chest heaved. Profanity spewed from his mouth.

She dropped the washcloth and sprang off the bed. Her heart fluttered as if she had run a race. "Forgive me. I'm so sorry."

Tremors wracked the man's body. "Get out."

"I didn't mean to hurt you." She backed toward the door. "What do you need?"

"Sleep. Now, leave."

When her fingers touched the doorframe, she turned and sprinted back down the hall, ignoring the painful boomerang in her head.

Jumping into bed, she pulled the sheet over her body and wrapped herself into a ball. The feeling of the man's thigh tingled on her hand. She opened and closed her fist, but the sensation would not disappear. It was etched into her nerves and etched into her memory.

Her hand had touched his thigh, and then, nothing.

The rest of his legs didn't exist. They were gone.

What had happened to cause such a deformity? Her arms closed in tight around her knees.

I want to go home.

2

Josephine bunched up her pillow and tried not to think of anything. Not swears from an injured man. Not the ache from her injury. Not the confrontation with her stepfather. Nothing. Going home and getting back to work on her patterns was her responsibility.

"Water girl?"

She bolted into a sitting position and immediately regretted the sudden movement. She knew that haggard voice. Had she misunderstood the summons? She listened intently as if for the squeak of a mouse.

The man called to her again.

Oh, why did she listen? She knew why. Few were the nights her mother didn't call out from pain.

Her hand trembled slightly as she poured a glass of water. For a few minutes, she stared at the glass. The last time she played nurse the man had shouted at her. She didn't even know what some of the names meant. Looking at the ceiling, she said, "Remember this, Lord."

A quick peek into the hallway showed no sign of a wayward Mrs. Prescott. She shuffled carefully toward the stranger's door and positioned herself near the entrance to his dimly lit room.

"You came," he said, his voice strangled and

rough.

"I came to ease my conscience and to get some sleep." She offered him the water glass. He took it from her but didn't drink.

"I need two white pills." He pointed to a metal box on top of a tall armoire. "My caretaker's sick."

"I can't," she said. "I'll get in trouble."

"It's just an aspirin, Runt. Read the label."

How dare he insult her? Josephine crossed her arms, crushing all the mail-order bows on her gown, and drew to her full height—five feet nothing.

"I am not a runt."

"Short hair, short body, short legs, you're a runt. Now, get me that pill." He pushed his body higher against the headboard. "Do it," he demanded. "I hurt." His tone softened.

An upholstered chair sat next to the armoire. Couldn't he—? Her hand tingled with memory. *I didn't touch a long leg.* She hesitated as her pulse hammered against her veins.

Do it. Don't. Do it. Don't. Do it. Don't.

She met his gaunt-eyed gaze and carefully climbed onto the chair. The last thing she needed was to fall and hit her head again. She reached for the metal box and opened it. Rows of bottles and a stack of syringes filled the little chest. She picked up a copper tinted bottle from the left-hand side.

"It's on the right," he coached. "Don't mess with that bottle. The doctor counts those narcotics. If you give me any more of that tonight, you may not get out of here alive."

She ignored his threat. "I may be unsteady, but I do believe I could make it out the door before you could make it out of bed."

"Don't worry. I'm cranky when I don't get much sleep."

When wasn't he cranky? She picked up the bottle he indicated and recognized the brand. Her mother used these for pain. She shook out two white pills and placed the bottle back in the box before tidying up the row and closing the metal latch.

She handed him the pills. He drained the water glass. When he had finished drinking, she reached out to take the glass from him.

"What do you want?"

"The glass."

He did not move. His hand clutched the glass, resting it on top of the blanket near his thigh.

"I need the glass." Heat, blood, and embarrassment rushed to her cheeks. She braced for a struggle to get the crystal back. "I don't want it missing from my room. The other one either. I don't want Mrs. Chambers to think I'm a thief." Her bottom lip quivered.

"Stop that. He moved the glass away from his thigh. "Take it. I don't know where the other one went. Search if you like."

She inched her hand closer toward the glass. "You won't curse again?"

He shook his head.

Her gaze never wavered from his unshaven face until her fingers were wrapped around the prize. She grabbed the glass and wedged it under her armpit for safety. She skimmed the room for the other cup, but she didn't see it.

The man flinched as though he had taken another drink bath.

She glanced to where his legs should have formed

two long lines underneath the sheets. The covers lay flat against the bed.

"It's not polite to stare." His lifeless eyes were as empty as the crystal glass.

"I didn't mean to. I've just never seen such an injury." Or felt it.

His brow furrowed. "Are you ignorant of the war? Those are my legs after the Germans tried to blow up my trench."

And like the night before, he bent forward, swearing, and curling his hands into fists. He beat the bed as tears trickled down the sides of his face.

"Where does it hurt? I'll get someone." She didn't know what she was saying. She would say anything because tomorrow she knew she would be home, sleeping with her sister, and this man would be a mile away.

"No," he called out, "don't get anyone. It's my feet."

She had to have misunderstood. He had no feet.

Chanting breaths filled the room. "They hurt even though they aren't there. Funny isn't it?"

"Not really." She didn't like to see people suffer.

Slowly, he unfurled his body.

"I should go," she said. "My forehead aches. Not as bad as your feet though. I think." She stepped backward.

"Belleau Wood."

The words sounded foreign to her. "Is that your name?"

"No." He laughed and shook his head. "It's a battle. I'm Geoff Chambers."

She kept her jaw from hitting the rug. From what her sister had said, Geoff Chambers was broad, handsome, and charming. Her cheeks grew warm. "I'm—"

"Josephine Nimetz. Town seamstress. I know because the maid complained about making up the guest room."

"Oh, well, I won't be here long." She'd leave first thing in the morning and not be any more of an imposition to the Chambers.

Geoff leaned forward, holding himself upright with his arms. "At Belleau, the Germans tried to pick us off as we took back the forest. A shell detonated near my position. Mangled my limbs. That's why I couldn't get those pills."

Josephine's mouth gaped. "You were at the front? And survived an explosion?"

"Yeah, if you can call it that. At first, the medics left me for dead. Blood covered my body. Wasn't all my own, either. They didn't know I was alive until they heard me moan." A lopsided smirk puffed out his cheek. "I guess I'm good at that, except on a battlefield the dead can't complain about the noise."

"My mother said we're winning the Great War."

"People still die, lose their lives." He looked down at the foot of the bed. "If your mother's right, who knows, maybe we'll pop a cork before the end of December. That would make 1918 a heck of a year."

He leaned his head against his wooden head rest. "I'm tired. The aspirin must be working." His eyes closed. "Good night, Runt."

"It's…"

A snore reverberated from the pillow. Fake or real she did not know.

She backed out of the room, still holding the crystal glass. Her soul grew heavy thinking about

Geoff Chambers and all the men the war had hurt or killed or maimed. Geoff didn't lose his life on the battlefield, but he would never be the same again. His painful disfigurement made her heart ache like a real live pin cushion.

Josephine climbed into her big, fluffy bed and tried to put the tormented man in the other room out of her mind. She glanced around the bedroom at the opulent decorations. Her damp row house couldn't compare to this luxury. If only she could afford a respectable home with nice furnishings for her mother. She didn't want to worry if the department store received a new shipment of dresses. She didn't want to worry if her fingers seized up. She didn't want to worry.

She shut her eyes. Someday a mansion would be waiting for her. Someday. Somewhere.

3

Morning finally came, bringing with it the sunlight Josephine so desperately desired. She was in the Chamberses' glorious mansion, and her throbbing head and stiff neck reminded her how she got there. *Ivan.* She would check on her mother first chance she got.

Someone tapped at her door.

Josephine sat and straightened the sheets.

"Good morning, Josephine. How are you feeling?" Mrs. Chambers's voice was like a heralding angel. "You gave us quite a scare yesterday."

Smiling a finally someone-I-know smile, she said, "I'm fine, ma'am." She admired Mrs. Chambers's crepe de chine dress, the gold buckles on her heeled pumps, and her silky tan stockings. "Are you well?" *Or did Geoff's wailing keep you awake?*

"You don't have to be so formal with me. I'll have Mrs. Prescott bring you something to eat."

"Thank you. Now that I'm up, I am hungry and ready to get back to work." Josephine sprang forward in the bed. "Your box!" Her head throbbed a warning. "The gloves. They fell."

Mrs. Chambers sat down next to Josephine and took her hand. "I have the gloves and handkerchief."

Her voice cracked. "Terrible things have happened. I can scarcely speak of them. When my husband and I came across you lying there in our yard." She paused and blew out a breath. "Marshal Dorsey will be coming in a little while to talk with you. You must speak freely."

The marshal? Did Ivan try to get money from her mother? "Is my mother all right?"

"She's at home. Not ill. You'll understand after you speak to Mr. Dorsey."

Mrs. Chambers patted Josephine hand. "Enjoy your breakfast. We have one of the best cooks in all of Alaska."

"I will. Thank you." She kept her answer calm even though a knot cinched her stomach. Was she in trouble with the law? Was Ivan?

When Mrs. Prescott came to pick up the tray, male voices could be heard in the hallway. Mr. Chambers and Marshal Dorsey entered her room. Josephine tugged her covers up around her chest.

"Josephine Nimetz." The marshal walked toward the bed. "You're a sight for these eyes. Mind if I sit right here?" He indicated a spot near the edge of the bed.

She nodded and glanced at Mr. Chambers. He looked stately, dressed in a well-tailored, vested suit, but what he held in his hand caught her attention most of all. He clutched a crystal glass. A glass from the set by her bed.

Her heartbeat rallied. She had brought two glasses into Geoff's room. But she had only retrieved one.

"I'm not going to mince words," the marshal began, rubbing the stubble of a beard. "I need to have some answers about what happened yesterday. Did someone give you those bruises on your neck? That bump?"

She smoothed the sheets on the bed and said nothing, contemplating what would happen if she told the marshal that her stepfather had caused her fall. She didn't want to think of what Ivan might do to her if she told. He had a quick temper and a quicker hand. Her mother needed his salary from the mine, even if there wasn't much left after he bought his drink and placed his bets. If her stepfather was put in jail, the money would stop for good, not to mention her family would be shamed with the scandal.

"Josephine, I need the truth," the marshal coaxed. "How did this injury happen? Did you stop to talk to anyone?"

She inspected the double-stitched hem of the bed sheet with her thumbnail. "I don't talk to strangers."

"Then you knew this person?"

Should she confess? Or say she slipped? She didn't want Ivan to miss anymore paydays at the mine. *Tell the truth.* Didn't her mother say the truth always came out anyway? The marshal must know something because he was still stationed on her bed.

"He was drunk," she stammered.

"Who? I don't like guessing games." The marshal's bushy eyebrows arched high on his forehead. He moved closer to her, his broad shoulders dwarfing her petite frame.

"Please, I don't remember much." She twisted the bed linens into a sidewinding snake.

The marshal fidgeted, intensifying his lawman stare.

"Maybe we should come back," Mr. Chambers said. He rotated the glass in his hand.

Marshal Dorsey leaned in and adjusted his thick leather belt. "Don't make me get your mother. I don't want to drag her into this mess."

Fear and humiliation arm wrestled inside her chest. "My mind wasn't right after I fell."

Mr. Chambers shifted forward in his high-backed chair and reached toward the bed. "Who hurt you?" His tone was like a warm cup of hot chocolate.

She looked past the marshal to Mr. Chambers. "My stepfather, but it was an accident. He needed money."

"You don't need to be afraid of your stepfather anymore." The marshal's hand engulfed her shoulder. "We found him last night. He wasn't as fortunate as you. He's expired. Someone shot him."

"Dead? Ivan?" Her lips parted, opening and closing like a fish languishing on dry shore. She shook her head and thought of her mother. Tears welled in her eyes. "Does my family know?"

"I broke the news to your sister and mother this morning." The marshal squeezed her hand before he rose from the bed. "You have my sympathies." He acknowledged Mr. Chambers. "I'll see myself out."

She slouched against the solid headboard and studied the pattern of wood knots on the ceiling. The dam holding her tears started to crack, spilling salt water down her cheeks. She swept the wetness from her eyes. Missed droplets hung from her chin. She and her family would manage somehow. Ivan would be walking into the light. Or would he?

Mr. Chambers took the marshal's spot on the bed. "I'm sorry for your loss, Josephine." He set the glass on her nightstand. "I need to ask. Were you in my son's room last night? I'm not upset, but we don't like to leave glass by his bed. Anything sharp, for that matter. Geoff hasn't been the same since he returned from France."

Josephine used the bed sheet to dry off her face. "I didn't know. I heard him calling for water." She cleared her throat, trying to control the wobble in her voice.

"My son calls out often. Did he scare you?"

"No. I slept well." A half-truth. "I took care of Mr. Gilbertsen before he passed. He was bedridden and needed a lot of care."

"My apologies for the noise. We are in-between nurses. A replacement should arrive shortly." He stood and strolled toward the door. "We're trying to keep Geoff comfortable. It doesn't always work." Mr. Chambers's eyes glistened. "If there's anything I can do, please let me know."

"When will I be able to go home?" she asked, her body collapsing into the soft pillows.

"Soon. I'll have a driver take you. Dr. Miller would like to check your stitches again for signs of infection."

The moment the door closed, Josephine let a stream of pent-up tears dampen the pillowcase. She could not stop their flow, nor would she try. She wouldn't have to face her stepfather. Part of her was relieved, but part of her would miss him. He was a decent man when he wasn't drinking, although lately, that man rarely showed up. She buried her face in the sheets and mourned for the man who would never show up again.

After the doctor visited, Marty Hill drove her home in Mr. Chambers's Model-T. Josephine was surprised to see Mr. Hill in Juneau for he managed a mine on Douglas Island. Apparently, not well enough to keep her stepfather out of trouble.

Josephine opened the door to her home, content to be back with her mother and Ann.

"Josephine Primrose! What happened to your hair?" Her mother's rigid fingers slid from the top of Josephine's head down the side of her neck, narrowly missing her stitches. Pain shot to Josephine's collar bone as her mother rubbed a bruise left by her late husband.

She ducked out from under her mother's needling fingers and allowed the chauffeur, Mr. Hill, to enter. He looked as if he was leading a parade in his pin-striped suit and wide-brimmed hat.

"Doctor Miller got carried away with the scissors. But the Chambers took good care of me," Josephine said.

"My poor baby." Her mother gave her a one-armed hug. "Well, Mr. Hill, I didn't expect you to come out to Juneau from the island. I'm grateful to have my Josephine back though. Lord knows, she's my right arm."

Mr. Hill removed his hat. "I'm sorry for your loss, Mrs. Nimetz. Ivan will be missed at the mine. I'd like to give my condolences to the rest of the family if I may?"

Her mother rubbed her crooked right hand. "Father Demetriev is waiting at the cemetery. He's fitting the burial in before another funeral."

"May I escort you?" Mr. Hill offered.

"Just family." Mrs. Nimetz glanced at Josephine and started to sway.

"I'll relay your condolences to my sister." Josephine wrapped her arm around her mother for support.

"Thanks. I'm sure I can count on you." Mr. Hill winked and retreated out the door.

Josephine helped her mother into the living room.

Her sister, Ann, slipped into a raincoat without as much as a hello. "You should have let him drive us. I haven't had a finely dressed escort in a while."

"He isn't family," Josephine said. The last thing she wanted to do was answer any more questions about her meeting with Ivan, especially questions from his boss.

Mrs. Nimetz smoothed the re-sewn collar on Josephine's coat. "After all Mr. Chambers has done for us, the last thing we need to do is tie up his car all morning. It's a clear fifty-seven degrees. The short walk will do me good." She bent closer toward Josephine. "But we must get you a hat."

Josephine stayed in step with her mother's gait. Ann walked on ahead, blazing a path to the church. Josephine gently squeezed her mother's hand and breathed in the scent of pine sap from the fresh-cut logs loaded on the docks below.

"What else has Mr. Chambers done?" Josephine asked as they neared the town square.

"He bought the cemetery plot for us, even gave the man who found Ivan's body a week's wages not to say anything about the way he died." Her mother's lips thinned as she drew in a deep breath. "The newspaper said it was a heart ailment that killed him."

Josephine tucked a stray strand of hair under her hat. "How will we ever repay the Chambers for their kindness?"

"Kindness?" Ann whipped around. "Ivan worked in their mine for years. Look what it got him."

"But..."

"No buts, Josephine. You listen to me. The mighty Chambers didn't want publicity about one of their miners getting murdered. People would get to talking about their crazy son being to blame. If you hadn't opened your big mouth to Marshal Dorsey, he might have thought their son attacked you." Ann poked at the plum-colored bruises on Josephine's neck.

"That's not true." Josephine freed herself from her mother's arm and squared her shoulders, trying to gain an inch on her sister's height. "Geoff Chambers couldn't have knocked me down. Ivan came at me. He wanted my sewing money."

"Money?" Ann's head shot back. A shrill cackle split the gray sky. "He needed money and he went to you?"

A geyser of anger flared from the soles of Josephine's worn boots into her fisted hands. "I was delivering the accessories you forgot to put with Mrs. Chambers's gown."

"Girls, please." Mrs. Nimetz hobbled forward, separating her daughters. "There are people in the churchyard."

"No one can blame this mess on me," Ann said through gritted teeth. She patted the dirty-dishwater-blonde braids emerging from her sport hat.

Josephine glanced past her sister to the church where Father Demetriev stood near the gate to the cemetery. She gave the priest a we'll-be-there-soon wave. "Let's not keep the priest waiting."

Ann stomped her foot and rushed toward the church.

Josephine consoled her mother and longed for life to get back to normal—pre-death normal. Sewing machines and bolts of fabric never threw dagger-eyed tantrums. But now, with Ivan gone, they just might, for she'd have to sew twice as much, twice as fast to help support her mother.

4

Josephine folded her arms on her family's kitchen table and rested her head on her black cotton sleeves. Being angry at the dead was draining. Pangs of guilt fluttered in Josephine's chest as she accepted the neighbors' sympathies along with their sweet-smelling cinnamon bread. September 17 would go down in her diary as the longest day of the year even if the sun had already set.

Her back muscles ached as if she had pick-axed her way through a wall of granite. Maybe it was from the standing and hugging, maybe still from her fall, maybe—she didn't have enough emotion left to care. Her hearing must have been going, too. She thought she heard footsteps outside the door. Certainly, condolence visits were done for the night. A knock at the door startled her whole family.

Her mother straightened her skirt and stumbled to the door. Her passionless face brightened with an I-can't-believe-it's-you smile.

Mr. Chambers came into view.

"Mr. Chambers, do come in," her mother said. "To what do we owe the pleasure of your company?"

"I'm sorry to bother you at such a difficult time." Mr. Chambers rotated his hat in his hand like a waterwheel.

Ushering their guest to a small sofa, her mother struggled to get seated in her lounge chair.

"I'll heat some water for tea," Josephine said, leaving Ann and her mother to accept Mr. Chambers's condolences and answer any further questions about Ivan.

When she returned from the kitchen, she sat in a chair next to the loveseat. Mr. Chambers gave her a friendly nod all the while rubbing his palms together as if winter had set in. What had brought him out to the row houses so late?

"I don't mean to be forward." Mr. Chambers cast a glance in her direction. "I came about my son, Geoff."

"Oh." Josephine pictured Geoff's fragile state. Did she leave something in his room? Give him pills the doctor counted? "I hope nothing has happened?" She tried to keep her voice from cracking.

Mr. Chambers shook his head. "Geoff is going to be taking up residence at the Gilbertsens' hunting lodge on Douglas Island for the winter. We thought it would be best for his health."

"I hear the lodge is very nice," Mrs. Nimetz said, edging out of her seat.

"It is," Mr. Chambers agreed. "Mr. Gilbertsen updated the plumbing before he died. Montgomery Ward mail order, I think. Being on the island will shelter my son from the influenza. It's only a matter of time before the sickness comes here. In his state, we can't risk an illness."

"I didn't realize he could live alone," her mother said encouragingly.

"He can't. He needs a caregiver." Mr. Chambers paused. "I know it's a sad time for your family, but

Josephine spoke of her experience with the Gilbertsens. And Mrs. Gilbertsen has sung Josephine's praises. It seems she was a superb junior nurse when Mr. Gilbertsen was ill, and I am in need of a nurse."

"My sister is not a nurse," Ann corrected.

"Close enough." Heat rushed to Josephine's face. "I assisted Mrs. Gilbertsen when her husband had pneumonia. They stayed in town to be close to the doctor, but I cared for his day-to-day needs."

Her mother's brows V'd like a flock of gulls. "Josephine helped, though she came home at night."

Mr. Chambers leaned so far forward she thought he was going to pray on bended knee.

"Geoff needs daily care. I would compensate your daughter well Mrs. Nimetz, at least one and a half times your husband's salary, and it's temporary. Geoff will come home next summer. God willing."

"Absolutely not," Ann commanded everyone's attention. "With all due respect, Mr. Chambers, I hear your son is shell-shocked. That lodge is on the other side of the island. What if there's an incident?"

Josephine bristled at the insult to Geoff. He could be difficult, but he didn't seem crazy.

Mr. Chambers rested his elbows on his knees. He stopped wringing his hands, and instead, laced them into his graying brown hair. "I assure you, Mrs. Nimetz—"

"Geoff is in his right mind. I met him this morning." *Very early this morning.* Josephine stood and crossed her arms. She would not see Mr. Chambers humiliated by Ann's run-amok mouth. "When did you say the position ends?"

"June." Mr. Chambers's voice rose like an Easter hymn. "We expect Geoff will come home then."

"She is my youngest," her mother said. "Who will help me sew?"

Ann rubbed her mother's back.

Josephine glimpsed her mother's arthritic hands curved in unnatural ways. She didn't help her mother sew; her mother helped her tailor dresses and suits. With the new department store in town, business had evaporated. She turned to Mr. Chambers. Indebtedness swelled in her chest. The Chambers had taken care of her after her fall. Could taking care of Geoff really be that bad? "Until June you say?"

"Only 'til June," Mr. Chambers said. His fingers brushed the edge of her sleeve. "Very few people who meet Geoff visit again. You did," he added softly.

An acceptance caught in Josephine's throat. Ann was capable of taking care of her mother. The money would cover expenses, even the cost of her mother's medication.

"I would be forever grateful to you, Josephine. Mrs. Prescott is too busy to take care of Geoff while performing her household duties. And the stress on my wife and young son…" Mr. Chambers stopped to compose himself. "Bradley is only ten. My wife doesn't think Geoff's situation right now is appropriate for a young boy to see. I had other arrangements made, but they fell through. I don't know what else to do. I'm at a dead end."

Josephine's pulse raced. Red, itchy blotches erupted on her hands. Her family waited for her answer as if she was declaring the war to be won.

"What about us?" Ann asked, filling silence. "My sister would be leaving the family business to take care of your son. She is almost eighteen. People will talk. And we are already dealing with enough gossip."

Her mother nodded. "It has been difficult for us."

Mr. Chambers addressed her mother. "I assure you; I will use my status in this community to suppress any slander against Josephine or your family. People who understand my son's injuries realize he is not out chasing women."

If that wasn't an understatement, she didn't know what was. Geoff sprinting? Josephine tried to glean any indication of her mother's wishes before replying to Mr. Chambers. Her mother's face was as plain as bed linen.

She turned toward Mr. Chambers. "I have taken care of someone who was ill, but pneumonia is different than your son's injuries," she paused not wanting to say anything too personal about Geoff. "The salary is generous." She faked a charm school smile as her mother's words came back to her about taking much-needed medication, 'only at night.' Not anymore. Was she out of her mind?

She cleared the cobwebs from her throat. "I accept. At least I won't have to sneak a peek at the fashions in Mr. Rickteroff's store window to see our competition."

The grooves in Mr. Chambers's forehead vanished. He shot to his feet and grabbed her hand. "Thank you," he said, hugging her briefly. "My family is in your debt."

Josephine's mother settled back in her chair and wiped her eyes with a handkerchief.

"You are a man of great wealth," Ann said, diverting Mr. Chambers's attention. "Surely, doubling my stepfather's wages is the proper thing to do for Josephine and our family?"

"Very well. Your sister does have experience with the infirm. I'll send the car for her in the morning."

Josephine's mind spun like a top. "I'll need time to say good-bye. And finish a customer's blouse."

Mr. Chambers clasped Josephine's hand in his. "One o'clock then?" He slowly released his grip. "I won't forget your sacrifice."

Josephine nodded. "I will do my best." She hoped that would be good enough.

Her mother accompanied Mr. Chambers to the door, sending regards to his wife and sons.

Josephine's stomach hollowed as if Mr. Chambers had snatched her confidence before fading into the night. She recalled her encounters with Geoff Chambers. A chilled night shiver wracked her bones. If only Ivan hadn't gambled his paycheck. If only her mother hadn't been arthritic. If only she had earned some of Mr. Chambers's money before Ivan had need of it.

Her mother wrapped her in a hug. "You are special, my blessing," she whispered. "With your position, our family will make it through this nightmare."

Josephine embraced her mother and buried her face in her mother's braided hair. *Will I be able to make it 'til June? Will Geoff?*

She didn't want to leave her mother and sister, but she didn't want to disappoint Mr. Chambers. Her stitches ached as she remembered her fall in the woods. The Chambers had taken her into their home and tended to her injuries. How could she refuse to take care of their son? Her own compassion had brought her face to face with Geoff. And Geoff did need a nurse. Disappointing Mr. Chambers would weigh upon her heart. Disappointing Mrs. Chambers would cost her a customer. Her best customer.

The more she thought about it, the more it seemed like death was the only way she could get out of this arrangement. Geoff Chambers's death or something short of her own.

5

At 12:55 PM the following afternoon, Josephine paced by the door with her sewing basket and a pair of boots in hand. Ann carried the embroidered bag that held her clothes and toiletries. Her mother sat at the kitchen table, lips quivering, trying not to break down and cry.

With every measured step, Josephine convinced herself she could do this job. Geoff was immobile and slept most of the day, just like Mr. Gilbertsen. Geoff had an established routine just like Mr. Gilbertsen. Geoff wasn't fond of baths just like Mr. Gilbertsen.

When the Model-T came into sight with Mr. Hill at the wheel, Ann started bobbing like a toddler in need of a potty break. There wasn't much to load into the car, but Ann found ample time to converse with Mr. Hill.

"It's only a few months," Josephine said, trying to console her mother.

Ann hugged Josephine good-bye. "Write if you need anything. Douglas Island isn't too far away." The oh-yes-it-is expression on her sister's face made Josephine's stomach twine into a square knot.

Conversation halted when Mr. Hill handed her mother an envelope. It was mid-September, but Ann had coerced payment for the full month.

She slipped into the car and rested her arm on the black metal windowsill of Mr. Chambers's Model-T while her mother and Ann waved good-bye. Wisps of dark brown hair tickled her face as Mr. Hill sped away, merging onto Juneau's main street. The sight of the Chamberses' brick mansion hollowed her bones.

Visions of popping open the door and racing back down the hill kept playing in her mind. *I can do this. I have to.*

Mrs. Prescott came out to meet them, pursing her lips at the mud that had splattered on the shiny black paint.

"Follow me, Miss Nimetz. I will show you where to put your things."

Josephine slung her bag over her shoulder, picked up the sewing basket and boots, and followed the housekeeper to her assigned room.

"Is that all you brought?" Mrs. Prescott asked.

"Yes," Josephine said, entering the familiar room with the big, cozy bed.

"You will need provisions for your stay at the lodge?" Mrs. Prescott scanned Josephine's body, starting at her feet and ending with a stern expression aimed at her wind-blown hair. "Mr. Chambers has asked me to procure some items before you leave."

Josephine didn't want to seem greedy or forward, but having something to pass the time when Geoff was occupied or sleeping might make her stay bearable.

"If it wouldn't be too much trouble, some fabric for sewing and stationary would be nice. I don't expect to have much free time, but some reading material might come in handy. Some women's magazines with stories."

"Very well, but before I leave, there are a few things you need to know. Have you ever given a shot?"

"A shot?"

"An injection with a needle. A syringe."

"No, I haven't. Dr. Miller took care of the injections for Mr. Gilbertsen."

"Well, you'll learn. The nice thing about morphine, if you make a mistake they don't feel it for long."

What happened when the patient did feel the pain?

Mrs. Prescott handed her a manual Doctor Miller had sent listing the drugs Master Chambers needed and at what times they should be given. Written at the top of the page was a stern warning never to leave any sharp instruments in close proximity to the patient.

The housekeeper also gave her a pamphlet on wound care, a small box of recipes—Geoff's favorites— and an address book. The instructions ended with an encouraging word to do the best in an emergency but to not take any dismal outcomes to heart.

Josephine put everything on the nightstand by her bed, moving the pitcher and glasses to the dresser so she would have room for her instruction manuals. She sat for a moment on the bed and rubbed her forehead. How did Mrs. Prescott expect her to learn everything in such a short time?

With company expected in the afternoon, she was ushered into Geoff's room to help him get ready. Was this a test of her preparedness? No one was lined up at the door to take her job. She decided to do her best and pray for a miracle.

"Well, if it isn't the runt," Geoff said as if he was announcing a sale at Rickteroff's store.

Mrs. Prescott excused herself and closed the bedroom door.

"Hello, Mr. Chambers." She tried to sound calm and cheerful even though her heart lub-dubbed against her chest, quaking her blouse.

"Is my father here?" He glanced toward the door. "Call me Geoff when we're in private. You make me feel old otherwise. How young are you anyway?"

"I'll be eighteen next month."

He snickered as if remembering a joke. "I should get paid to babysit you. Get over here, Runt, and stop standing in the corner. I'm being seen today."

She walked toward the bed. Geoff sat propped against the headboard like before. When she started to sit down, he grabbed her arm, pulling her face into the warmth of his wet cardboard breath. Her mouth clamped shut.

"Don't sit on my bed unless I show you where to sit. Lord help me if you squeeze my legs again, I might just snap your neck on accident."

Her eyes widened then relaxed. She didn't dare look away. He had to believe she didn't scare easy. But she did.

She tugged her arm out of his grasp. "Fine."

"Now, go get me a pair of pants and a shirt out of that armoire."

Her trembling fingers rattled the pulleys on the armoire doors. She managed to find a white oxford shirt and a pair of tan pants. Force of habit, she examined the construction of the pant legs. The right leg was longer than the left.

"What are you looking at, Runt? Never seen a pair of pants before?"

"They're uneven." She positioned herself

34

cautiously on the end of the bed.

"I'm uneven."

"Why do you want people to notice that?"

"I don't. And stop asking me stupid questions. I can't believe the only person my father could find to care for me is a girl who took care of an old man." The palms of his hands shot to his head. "I own a darn gold mine and a hunting lodge, but I can't have a proper nurse? I'm not a lunatic."

"I never said you were." She emphasized her innocence.

After hanging his clothes over the bedpost, she hurried toward the door. Pebbles of pride tumbled down her slumped shoulders. Tears pooled in her eyes from his criticism. *Stop it. Stop it. Stop it.*

"Wait. Where are you going?"

She halted in front of the door but didn't turn around. Her cheekbones warmed like a stoked fire. She wouldn't give him the satisfaction of seeing her humiliating glow. Fleeing the mansion crossed her mind. Could she leave even though her service for September had already been paid?

"I'm sorry. You're not stupid. If you want to even the pants go ahead. I have an important guest coming today, and I need you to stay." A strangled sigh cut through the silence. "I'd like to look presentable. If that's possible."

She opened the door but didn't look at him. The air in the hallway smelled like dew-laden May grass.

"My sewing basket's in my room. I'll need to iron the material afterward, so why don't you wash up."

"I give the orders," he said. "Remember that."

She left, grateful for the reprieve from Geoff and for sewing-related work.

When she had finished altering his pants, she returned to his room and faced the wall while he tried them on. Grunts rose from the bed.

"OK, how do I look?" he asked, giving his shirt one last tuck.

The ends of his stumps hung off the bed. She tried not to stare, but she wanted to check her hurried stitching.

"Not bad. You should pass inspection." She pushed the wheelchair closer to the bed. He actually chuckled at her reply.

Geoff took hold of the chair's arms and slowly lifted his body onto the seat, leaving blood stains visible on the bed linens.

The scarlet streaks held her attention. "Are you bleeding?"

"Bed sores. A curse for the immobile." He tried to flatten a cowlick that sprung from his forehead. "Forget the sheets. How's my hair?"

Her nose wrinkled at the bold part down the center of his head.

"Don't look at me like that. What's wrong?"

"Nothing. It's just that I prefer a part to the side. It's less harsh, but if—"

"Fix it." He handed her a comb from the nightstand.

She swept his hair across his forehead and caught a whiff of his body odor. The combination of his medication and his perspiration formed a stale laundry scent.

"When was the last time you bathed?" she asked, sweeping his brown hair behind his ears.

His spine straightened.

"It's none of your business."

"It will be." She moistened her fingers to tackle his stubborn cowlick.

"Are you telling me I stink?"

"Not a stink. It's more of a sick person's smell. Do you have some scented shaving water?"

"Hand me a blade, and I'll put some on after I take off this stubble. There's a shaving kit by the medicine box." He snapped his fingers.

She did not move. Her gaze danced around the room until she spied an orange on the nightstand. Walking around the back of his chair, she picked up the fruit and scored it with a fingernail. She held it to his neck and gave a quick rub.

"Get that off of me," he shouted, bumping her arm.

Mrs. Prescott knocked on the door, interrupting his tantrum and announcing the arrival of Mr. Brice Todd. A stout stranger waited with Mrs. Prescott.

Geoff wheeled his chair toward the door. "I'll meet you at the bottom of the stairs."

She excused herself. She hadn't thought about how Geoff or his chair, for that matter, would get down to the main floor. She made a mental note to add that to her caregiver list.

Waiting near the bottom step, half-hidden by the railing, she tried not to notice the man carrying Geoff down the stairwell like a vaudeville ventriloquist's dummy. When Geoff was settled in the chair, he took control of the large wooden wheels, and she followed behind, grinning when she caught the scent of orange zest.

The guest, Mr. Todd, waited in an embroidered armchair, drumming his fingernails on a marble-topped table. He jumped to his feet when Geoff approached.

Josephine concentrated on the path in front of the wheelchair, trying not to stare at the handsome blond visitor. He wasn't too tall, just shy of six feet, but his forget-me-not blue eyes were the prettiest she had ever seen on a man. Geoff's blue eyes were darker, more of a bluish-gray, and they didn't sparkle with life like the gems in this man's eyes.

"You are the picture of health today," Brice said, extending his hand to Geoff. "And who is this young lad at your disposal?"

"My new caregiver. Josephine Nimetz." Geoff accentuated her first name.

"Excuse me, young lady. I couldn't see your dress behind the chair. With the short hair, I just assumed."

"Don't trouble yourself, Brice. She understands."

"I was expecting your brother to accompany you." Brice scanned the hallway.

"Bradley's in San Francisco visiting family or something." Geoff swung his hand out as if swatting a fly.

"Nimetz." Brice rubbed his smooth, cleft chin. "You have an older sister."

"Yes, sir." Josephine gripped the handles on Geoff's chair. She didn't expect to be drawn into the conversation.

"I believe she was a year ahead of Geoff and me. Ann, is it?"

"Yes, sir." She casually wiped her hands on a part of her dress hidden from view. Had Brice read the newspaper article about Ivan's death? Thankfully, no mention came of her family's misfortune.

"And you live in town?"

"Yes, sir."

Brice finally turned his attention back to Geoff.

"I'm jealous of the stimulating conversation you'll be having at the lodge."

The men laughed.

She ignored Brice's humor. If he wanted conversation, he shouldn't have asked her yes or no questions.

"Excuse me." Josephine walked off to admire an oil painting of a heavily side-burned gentleman and to eavesdrop without being noticed.

"My father told you then? About the Gilbertsen lodge?" Geoff said.

"He mentioned it. The change of scenery and fresh air should help with your recovery."

"Or put me in an early grave?"

"Oh, come on," Brice said. "You can't believe everything the doctor says. I've known you for years, and I can't recall anything you can't do except maybe sweet talk a certain Christine to go out with you."

Geoff gave a shared-secret chuckle. "That was a long time ago."

Was Christine Geoff's former lover? Talk of a girl made her turn from the oil painting and inspect a fern with fronds she could hide behind and still glimpse the men.

"I saw her the other day," Brice added, "with her husband. Funny, I thought Christine would marry someone tall, like you." Brice's eyes widened when he realized what he had said.

The room fell silent.

Geoff carved his armrest with his thumbnail.

"You'll have to come visit us at the lodge."

"Don't know if I'll make it this year. I'm taking some time away from my studies to travel." Brice crossed his legs and grasped his shoe as if it would fling across the room if he let go. "My folks don't want me living back east until this influenza blows over."

"You're not leaving a woman out east, are you?" Geoff gave up on his wood carving and settled his hands in his lap.

"One, but she's very studious. Probably won't even miss me."

"When you're done traveling, you can tell me all about it." Geoff shifted restlessly in his chair.

"The trip or the woman?"

"Both." Geoff leaned closer to Brice. "It's not like I'll have much to tell."

Josephine could have sworn Geoff indicated her somehow. It wasn't exactly fair that Brice got to travel to the lower forty-eight while she was going to be stuck at the lodge with Geoff. But then, Brice had money and she didn't. Not yet, anyway.

Brice didn't stay long. He was mindful of the packing that had to be done and the steamboat trip the next day.

Geoff kept to himself the rest of the night.

She ate a cold, late dinner in her room before checking in on Geoff.

"Would you like a bath?" Her voice hit a soprano's note as if she was coaxing a mud-caked boy into the tub. She had sponge-bathed Mr. Gilbertsen, but Geoff's body needed a good soak.

"No. Maybe tomorrow." He lay in bed, his back toward her.

"I have your morphine."

"About time." He tugged off the sheet, exposing his underwear and upper thighs as if it was no big deal.

It was a big deal to her. She had never seen a young man in his underwear before.

She swabbed Geoff's upper-thigh with alcohol careful not to linger too long on his leg. The pungent vapors stung her eyes and nostrils. Pulling Geoff's skin taut, she breathed deeply and blew on his skin, praying he wouldn't shout or jerk while she emptied the syringe.

"One...Two..."

Biting on her lip, she plunged the needle into his muscle.

Geoff flinched.

"Oops."

"What the heck did you say that for?" His head careened backward trying to see the injection site.

She swallowed hard. A piece of lip flesh slithered down her throat. "It bent." She removed the needle and held a piece of gauze over the tiny puncture wound.

"Next time don't say anything. Payback's when I remove your stitches."

"You won't," she stammered, capping the L-shaped needle on her third try. "The doctor will remove them."

"Doc Miller's not taking a steamer out to the lodge to pluck a few stitches. Yours won't be the first ones I've taken out. Might be the last."

"Don't tease about that."

"Who said I was kidding." His eyelids drooped. "Get some sleep. We haven't left Juneau, and you've already made your first mistake. Better not make many more." His words faded into the pillow.

She applied pressure to the mushroom of blood seeping from his ripped skin.

"Geoff," she whispered. "How many mistakes is too many?"

Only one of his eyes opened. "I'll let you know."

6

The *Lumberjack's Maiden* docked on the Gastineau Channel awaiting its cargo and passengers. Several men loaded crates and lumber onto the steamer. Josephine wheeled Geoff to the gang plank. Mr. Chambers had come to see them off. She searched the docks for signs of Ann or her mother, but it was early, and there weren't many people about town. Did her family even know the date and time of her departure?

A portly man shouted instructions to the crew coming aboard ship. Soon, she would be the one in charge of Geoff's household, but there wouldn't be anyone taking orders, except her.

The captain, with his leather-trimmed black cap, had a booming voice that echoed across several docks. He reminded her of Santa Claus with his wavy white hair, cropped frosted beard, and ripe berry cheeks. The sweet, fruity aroma from his pipe seasoned the morning air.

When there weren't any more men to instruct, the captain turned toward Geoff.

"Who do we have here, Master Chambers?" The captain's teeth held his pipe in check while his face lit up with a welcome-aboard smile.

"Josephine Nimetz." She extended her hand and

ignored Geoff's loud exhale.

"A young lady who speaks up. Glad to have you." The captain gave a firm shake. "I'm Captain Barrie, but you Miss, may call me Tubby."

"Call her Jo." Geoff turned his chair so the large rear wheels were closest to the ship.

"That's not my name."

"It is now. Josephine's too long to say more than once a day."

Two crewmen dragged the wheelchair up a wide plank and settled the chair onto the *Maiden's* deck. Geoff's body jostled arm rest to arm rest. She followed a short distance behind, making small talk with Mr. Chambers.

"Send word if you need anything." Mr. Chambers blotted his face with a handkerchief.

"I certainly will," she said, boarding the ship with a steadying hand from the captain. "But for now, we're packed up with more supplies than the general store."

She waved good-bye with closed-fingers and a slight bend to her palm, even, elegant. Inside she was screaming 'girl overboard.' Sitting in the rear of the *Maiden*, she watched the mountains sail by and surveyed their blanket of prickly pines for moose and bear. Geoff kept Tubby company while the captain steered the ship.

The *Lumberjack's Maiden* sailed down Gastineau Channel, rounded the tip of Douglas Island, and continued along Stephen's Passage before turning into an inlet. A long wooden dock split Mother Nature's half-circle right down the middle. Tubby docked the ship as if this was his home port.

The lodge was not the isolated pine box she pictured it to be. Her home in Juneau could have been its outhouse. The land leading up to the lodge was clear cut, but old-growth Spruce, Hemlock, and Sitka, stood guard at the edge of the forest. Taking care of Geoff in this log palace may not be so bad after all.

Men readied planks of wood and wheeled Geoff off the ship. A crewman helped propel the chair to the front porch. She followed, hopscotching from rock to rock, trying not to muddy the hem of her dress.

"How the heck am I going to get up those narrow steps? I paid good money for this lodge, and I can't even get to the door."

Her heart sped as if she had jumped every rock in the inlet. "I'll ask Tubby to have the men make a ramp."

First problem solved.

She patted Geoff's shoulder. He shrugged her away. Immediately, she eyed the front door to see if the wheelchair would fit. The door looked wide enough for a large rack of caribou antlers. Thank goodness the chair could roll inside.

Leaving Geoff on the porch to supervise the men unloading supplies, she entered her new home. The lodge was bigger and better than she had imagined. In the living room, a tooth-flashing head of a black bear silently roared above the stone fireplace, claiming ownership of its cozy territory. She figured the mount was one of Mr. Gilbertsen's trophies.

Two brown leather couches formed a sitting area around the hearth. She sank down into the cushions for a moment and noticed that with two couches, chairs, and a long wooden table, Geoff's wheelchair would not be able to fit between the furniture. If she moved the pieces farther apart, one couch would border the dining table, forming another wheelchair barrier.

She rose from her seat and inspected the bedroom that was to the left of the entry. The wide French doors brought her a sense of relief. Normally, she would admire the door's stained glass instead of surveying their width, but with Geoff in tow, she wanted to avoid another argument. An audible clack of her tongue accompanied a sigh when she spied the narrow doorway to the bathroom.

The whirr of his wheels on the wood floor sent a chilled shudder down her spine.

"This one's mine," Geoff said, wheeling into the bedroom. "Yours is up that steep staircase. Better hold the railing on your way down. We don't want any more accidents." He stressed his last word.

A pang of guilt weighed on her soul. *Dang needle.*

Tubby entered the bedroom.

"Is the ramp done?" she asked, hoping to check off a completed task from her caregiver list.

"Not yet." The edge to Geoff's voice was sharp enough to split wood.

She pictured Geoff cradled in the captain's arms and decided not to ask any more questions about how he got into the lodge.

"Twin beds?" Geoff gasped. "I haven't slept in a twin bed since I was a boy. What's next?" He gripped the arms of his wheelchair. "How am I supposed to use the toilet? Crawl?" He wheeled his chair over to the bathroom and pounded the molding with his fist. Veins raised on his neck and forearms.

"We'll push the beds together and I'll bring in a chamber pot. It will work." She tried to drown his simmering frustration. "I'm sure we can get the door widened."

"Not a problem," Tubby assured her. He carried

the nightstand to the corner of the room and pushed the beds together. "That's one problem solved."

Actually, it was the second.

With Tubby's help, she moved one of the living room couches into Geoff's room. It would be a convenient place for her to sleep if Geoff needed care during the night.

A crew member entered the bedroom and tapped her on the shoulder.

"Where do you want the hens, Miss?"

"Hens?" she repeated, hoping he'd clue her in and fast.

"For eggs." He rubbed his chin, cracking a cuspid-less grin.

"Is there a chicken coop out back?"

"No, Miss."

"They're not coming in my house." Geoff rubbed his palms together as if he was readying for a gun fight.

"Can you build a coop near the back door?" she asked. "If I let hens roam, the black bears will get fatter, and we'll get thinner."

The crew member chuckled. "I'll see what we can do."

She followed the coop expert through the kitchen and out the back door of the lodge. A small set of stairs led into the yard. A third problem.

"We'll need a ramp here, too," she yelled to the men splitting logs.

Josephine spent the rest of the afternoon unpacking crates, stocking the kitchen shelves and pantry, and piling dishes into cupboards she could reach without a chair. Geoff stayed out of her bobbed hair and ranted at the crew.

With hungry men scurrying about, she wasted no time stoking the wood and coal burning stove. She put biscuits in the oven to bake and made gravy on the stovetop. She didn't have time to be fancy, especially since she couldn't remember where she placed all the ingredients.

At mealtime, everyone sat comfortably around the large dining room table. Everyone except Geoff.

"Where's Mr. Chambers?" she asked Tubby.

Tubby shook out his napkin. "He went to his room. Said he wasn't hungry."

"That's a first. Men are always hungry."

Tubby laughed. "Can't argue with you there."

Geoff could.

After the blessing of the food, she dished up a plate and carried it to Geoff's room.

"You can't pass up my biscuits." She placed Geoff's dinner on the nightstand next to his wheelchair.

"I can if the gravy will wind up all over my pants." He adjusted his position and picked up his dinner. "My wheels won't fit under the table. Guess most hunters have two working legs."

"I'll see if Tubby can shave the tabletop down. Make an arch for the chair." There were so many adjustments that had to be made for Geoff. She hoped she and Tubby had conquered most of them. When the captain left, she would be alone to handle what came next. Whatever that may be.

After supper, she strolled with Tubby to the dock, leaving Geoff in front of the fireplace. She handed Tubby a small basket of biscuits and thanked him for his help.

"We'll return soon to check in on things," Tubby

said. "Got to get you supplied up for winter. Then, young lady, you can let me know if anything needs straightening out." He glanced up toward the lodge and gave her another knowing wink before boarding his ship.

Standing on the dock, she watched the *Lumberjack's Maiden* sail away into the setting sun. She waited, breathing in the fresh sea air. Stalling. Guilt tickled her conscience, but she couldn't handle another confrontation with Geoff. Her quota was full for the night. Meandering toward the front porch, she hit the steps—one, two, three, four.

After hanging up her coat, she took a deep breath and said the dreaded words. Words she had been lamenting all day.

"You need a bath." She braced for his response.

"Finish the dishes and boil some water. I don't think the tub has hot running water, and you're definitely not putting me in a deep freeze."

Victory. Or maybe not. How was the bath going to work?

She washed the dishes and envisioned different scenarios for bath time. Creaking pipes let her know that he had started his bath water. Shortly, she carried two kettles of boiling water into his bedroom.

The wheelchair stood empty next to the bed. Through the bathroom doorway, she saw Geoff propped against the side of the tub, bare-chested, wearing only his underwear.

"Can I come in?" she asked.

His head flopped backward and rested on the tub. "It's going to be kind of hard for you to assist me from way out there."

She laughed. She actually laughed. He laughed,

too.

Emptying the hot water into the tub, she asked, "How did you get in here?"

"I used my arms. Thank heaven the blast didn't blow off all my limbs." He motioned toward some cupboards. "We're going to need lots of towels."

Nodding, she asked, "How are we going to do this?"

"You're going to do as little as possible. I'll get a hold on the outside of this tub and stand myself up. You will lift my legs over the metal edge and back out again. I don't need you in between."

Thank heaven. Josephine ran her fingers through her locks, curling some behind her ears.

"Can you wash your hair?"

He scowled at her. "Of course I can."

"You'll need to soak those bed sores."

"Yes, doctor."

Geoff grasped the sides of the tub and lifted his body straight off the floor. "Up and over," he huffed, arm muscles bulging.

With her back to Geoff's chest, Josephine wrapped her arms around his legs and hoisted them into the tub. A shallow minefield of divots covered the skin beneath his left stump. Her ring finger sank into his flesh.

Dropping into the water, Geoff caused a small tidal wave to crest at the rim of the tub. A few drops splashed the side of her dress, hip level. She didn't mind the dampness. She had to take care of him.

"Anything else?" She laid a washcloth on the rim of the tub.

He shook his head. "Come when I call."

Josephine jogged upstairs to her bedroom and dead-dropped on to the hospital-white bedspread. She had a double bed all to herself—no Ann—a window with a view of the inlet, and a brand new Singer sewing machine, compliments of Mr. Chambers. She unpacked a few clothes before heading downstairs to check on Geoff.

"Are you decent?" She tapped on the bathroom door. Water gurgled down the drain.

"I'm always decent," he replied. "I'm covered if that's what you mean."

She entered the room and moved a bathmat closer to the tub.

While the water drained, he grabbed the metal sides and pressed his body into a stand. His soaked underwear dripped water onto the floor, onto the rug, and onto her shoes. She hurried to place a hand under each leg, avoiding Geoff's perturbed gaze. Her heart sputtered when she thought of what she might touch. Immediately, she shifted her hands toward the ends of his stumps.

Her foot slipped.

She fell.

Horizontal in the air, all she saw was tub and chest. Geoff's chest. Her body crashed into his damp skin, knocking him downward, and grinding his sores into the metal basin.

He screamed.

Shoulder bone constricted her windpipe. She gasped, "Sorry. So sorry. I slipped." Her breathy voice barked like a seal pup.

He clenched her arms.

Her heart thumped, threatening to burst through her ribs and her brassiere and her bodice. She stared at the bottom of the tub. Streaks of blood swirled from underneath Geoff's body.

Another mistake.
She met his piercing gray glare.
His grip tightened.
"Don't move."

7

She needed to get out of the tub. She needed to dry Geoff's skin and attend to his wounds. She needed a miracle. Geoff's hands were still wrapped around her arms. Arching her back, she lifted her neck, trying to glimpse the rim of the tub.

"If you drive my sores deeper into this metal, so help me, I'll—" His guttural shout shattered her eardrums.

Up and over the rim she flew, out of the tub, onto the floor.

She crawled back to the side of the tub and knelt beside it, trying to gather the right words. What could she say to him? The hatred in his eyes burned through her dress.

"You'll have to help me to bed." He panted. "I can't drag my butt on the floor."

He needed extra help because of her mistake. She was not blameless.

Throwing a towel over his legs, she lifted his stumps out of the tub and rested them on the palms of her hands on the floor. He crab-walked on his arms to the bed. She followed, hunched over, keeping up with his staggered rhythm.

When they reached the bed, he hoisted his torso

up on the mattress and flung himself, face first, into the pillows.

"Morphine," he breathed.

After righting his stumps, she sprinted up the stairs to her room and back down in less than a tick of a clock. Her hands shook with the tiniest tremble as she uncapped the needle, plunged it into his thigh, and released the drug. *Perfect.*

Geoff's head never left the pillow. He lay motionless, lifeless.

She removed the soaked underwear with its crimson stains. She had never seen a man's backside before; certainly not one with smashed bedsores and blood clots that looked like strawberry jam. Her stomach lurched at the sight.

"Sorry, Geoff. I'm so sorry."

A rumbling, like a low, far-off foghorn came from Geoff's mouth. Was it a snore? Or did he accept her apology?

She dabbed ointment on his wounds and covered them with gauze. Using the extra ointment, she massaged his legs.

He groaned.

"Does this hurt?"

"Feels different. Good pain." He snorted. "Like there's...guh...pain."

His breathing shallowed. A string of nasally grunts rose from the bed. He had fallen asleep.

She covered him with a blanket and crept up to her room. Snatching the bedspread, she settled into her new bed, the couch in Geoff's room. She kept watch, wide-eyed, with this-is-my-fault worry. What if it gets infected? What if he can't sit in his chair?

Over and over, her mind replayed the accident. *I*

have to do better.

"God, help me," she prayed. "Geoff is my patient."

When she opened her eyes, the clock struck 6:00 AM.

She washed, dressed, and fixed her hair. Useless. Not much could be done with her short hairdo. She raced outside where the hens waited for food. They didn't care if she stole their eggs as long as she scattered grain on the ground. She tied an apron around her gray gingham dress and set bread to rise before starting breakfast. Her cooking skills were adequate, but certainly not as seasoned as the Chamberses' private chef.

"What's in my chair?" He called from the bedroom. His voice could have been heard all the way to Stephen's Passage, but to her, his rant was like bright mountain sunshine.

She walked into his room. He laid on his side, facing the door, the blanket covering his lower-half.

"Foam. I was going to use it for a pillow, but it should help with the sores."

"Don't you mean craters?" He shifted in the bed. His teeth clenched, flaring his jawbone. "What's for breakfast?"

"Scrambled eggs and bacon."

"No toast?"

"I won't have bread baked 'til later."

Geoff struggled to sit up. She should offer to help him get dressed, but he was already undressed.

"Don't stand there staring at me. Hand me my clothes."

She licked her front teeth and tried to moisten her lips, but her tongue had turned to linen. "Um… do you need any assistance?" She placed his pants, shirt, and underwear on the bed.

"No, you've done enough." He waved her off like a bad odor.

She hurried back to the kitchen and prayed she could give Geoff the best care possible. That was her job.

Fifteen minutes later, he wheeled himself to the table.

"You should stay off your bu... backside for a while," she said, setting a plate of eggs before him. "You'll heal faster."

"How do you expect me to do that?"

"Lay on the couch. You could read a magazine or book."

"That sounds entertaining." He shoveled a fork full of egg into his mouth. "There's hunting books and Mrs. Prescott's *Woman's Home Companion*. That's not my cup of tea."

"Well then, I guess you'll have to watch me dust the furniture and clean the floor. With the crew in here yesterday, there are more tracks inside the lodge than out."

He grimaced and continued eating.

After breakfast, Geoff stretched out on the couch, facing the coffee table, with the book, *Rifles and Guns*.

On hands and knees, she washed the pine floor.

"Your parents are very nice," she said, trying to make conversation. Why shouldn't their time together be pleasant?

"She's not my mother."

"Oh, I just thought—"

"You don't think much do you?" He eyed her over the top of his book.

She wrung out the rag, giving it an extra twist,

trying to ignore his insult. He's in pain. *Pain because of my mistake.*

He slammed the book shut.

"My mother died when I was six. A year later, my father married Julia. Two years later Bradley was born. Now, here I lay watching a runt wash the floor because Julia's threatening to leave."

"Not because of you?"

His eyes widened. "She owes me. She has lived very well off the profits from the lumber and land my father owns. He would have none of it if it wasn't for the gold. Kat Wil Mine belonged to my mother's family."

"I didn't know." She regretted starting the conversation.

"Julia came from nothing. She was worse off than you."

"What do you mean by that?" Her voice rose to match his rant. A shiver rippled through her body. "My mother is the best seamstress around, and my stepfather, well, it's not nice to speak ill of the dead."

He flipped a page in his book. "Some dead deserve it."

She jumped to her feet and tossed the wet rag into the bucket. An all-out, drum-beating, banner-waving parade of anger marched across the inside of her chest. "My stepfather married a widow with two young girls, gave us his name, and put food on the table. It's not my fault riffraff from your mine put a bullet through him. I can sympathize with Julia. I've only been around you a couple of days, and I'd like to abandon ship."

"If you're trying to get rid of me, you sure did a bang-up job last night."

Her hand shook as she picked up the bucket and

turned to leave the living room. No use getting into a fight. Until Tubby returned, she was trapped.

"I need some fresh air," she said.

"Where are you going?"

Refusing to answer would bring another verbal assault. "There's a path out back, and I'm going to follow it."

"So help me, if you leave this lodge without me, your mother won't see another penny."

"We agreed on payment until June." Josephine's voice squeaked like a shy school girl being reprimanded in front of her class. "My mother is sick and a widow."

"Let's get one thing straight." He threw the book onto the coffee table. It sailed across the oak wood and over the edge. He didn't seem to care that she would have to pick it up later. "Our agreement is not about supporting your family. It's about me. And you taking care of my needs."

She put down the bucket. Her hand couldn't seem to hold the wobbly handle. Maybe a walk in nature was what they both needed. Maybe surveying his new property would take his mind off the pain. Maybe seeing God's creation would lift his spirits. No more rants, no more put downs, no more hurt feelings. At least not for the rest of the day.

She moved his wheelchair closer to the couch. "Hop on then." She braced the wheel with her boot.

He shifted himself into the chair, easing his weight onto the foam cushion. Snapping his fingers, he pointed to the stuffed bear's head above the fireplace. "Get the rifle down from its mount. Check to make sure it's loaded."

She froze. Mrs. Prescott had said no sharp objects.

She never mentioned guns.

"I'm not going into the woods without protection and neither are you." Geoff shook his finger at the gun. "I don't want the bears to mistake me for one big huckleberry."

This wasn't downtown Juneau. A trophy head of a black bear threatened the living room. She blew out a breath and relented. Standing on a stool, she retrieved the rifle, checked the chamber for bullets, and handed it to him.

He jerked it from her hand and laid it across his lap.

She pushed him through the kitchen, picking up a small woven basket that she wedged between his thigh and the arm of the wheelchair, much to his chagrin.

The path leading from the lodge had been cleared of bushes, ferns, and trees, but the roots of old-growth pines had risen to the surface, to freedom. Nature's sprawling hurdles reached up and grasped Geoff's wheelchair, showing no mercy to the dead-tree wheels.

"You're jiggling me too much," Geoff complained. "Keep this up and I'll need a transfusion." He grasped the wheel rims and cursed the basket.

She removed the obstacle. "You should really watch your swearing on such a glorious fall day."

She strolled on ahead admiring the fuchsia fireweed with its pulled-cotton seedlings while Geoff maneuvered the path's minefield grumbling with every I-can-do-this breath.

He lagged.

Her route ended at a creek. A blissful creek fed by a waterfall. The churning white water threw itself over a rock cliff and hugged the granite on its way down to earth. Mist cooled the air, the plants, and her face.

Geoff came alongside her.

"This is wonderful. We should put a bench out here," she said.

"I come with my own seating." He opened and closed his hands as if they had gone to sleep.

Red indentations marred his palms. Guilt hollowed her stomach. No matter what, she would push him back to the lodge. She didn't need his hands butchered like his bottom.

"Ah, it seems the bears have left you some huckleberries." Marching off the path to a bush brimming with dark-blue berries, she popped a few in her mouth. "They're almost too ripe and definitely too sweet for you." She tossed a berry at him to lighten his mood.

His head jutted forward like a trained seal in a circus. He caught the berry with his mouth, swallowed it, and grinned.

"Don't miss and stain that beige shirt." She tossed him another berry.

And another.

Both caught.

And eaten.

Clapping, she said, "I've never seen anyone catch three in a row before."

"There's not much to do in a trench." His smile vanished. His gaze pinned her skirt to the nearest spruce. He lifted the rifle from his lap. Slowly. Expertly.

"Come here," he commanded. "And quickly."

How could she move with a bullet aimed at her shoulder? Or was it her heart?

8

She stared at the rifle. He wouldn't shoot. Would he? Were the rumors Ann heard true? He was crazy. Shell-shocked. Bright spiraling lights like the wave of centipede legs blurred her vision, casting a halo around Geoff, the chair, but not the rifle. The barrel remained a vivid bronzed-black vision.

"Now, Jo."

The tuning fork hum in her ears distorted his voice. Scrambled eggs from breakfast scorched her throat. Gagging, she covered her mouth and forced herself to swallow.

The huckleberry bush rustled.

An animal became visible. Was it a wolf? It looked like a wolf, but it had auburn streaks in its pewter mane, a leather band around its neck, and no fierce growl.

She stepped toward Geoff, never losing eye contact with the animal.

"Hurry, I've got a clean shot."

Her knees were limp as cooked dumplings. She imagined fangs ripping into her flesh.

Step toward Geoff.

The beast continued its approach. It stopped and sat on its haunches.

"Shift to your left. I don't want to hit you." Geoff's voice was eerily calm.

She pictured the wolf's carcass and the blood and the scavengers.

"Do any of our neighbors have a dog?" she half-whispered.

"Neighbors? Are you insane? We have no neighbors. Listen to me."

"Don't shoot it. I think it lives here."

"There are a lot of animals that live here. We don't need any pets. That beast could devour a runt like you in no time." The echo off the rock cliff agreed with his arguments.

"Please Geoff. If I walk back to you, and it doesn't follow, don't shoot it." She met his stare, and it faltered for a second. "Please?"

"Start walking."

She moved, slow as a Sunday stroll, to his side and gripped the arm of his wheelchair.

The beast stayed put. Its tail whacked the bush, back and forth, knocking a few berries to the ground.

Geoff raised the rifle to his cheek. His finger squeezed the trigger.

"Don't," she screamed, knocking the stock against his face.

A shot rang out.

The animal scurried into the woods.

He thrust the butt of the rifle into the foam cushion. "Why did you do that?" he shouted, swinging his fist in the air.

She ducked even though his knuckles didn't come close to hitting her. She'd had plenty of practice dodging Ivan's outbursts.

"I could have shot you by accident." He rubbed

his reddening cheek. "What would I tell Tubby?" He slumped in the chair and winced. "Huh? What would I say when I handed him your rotting corpse?"

He didn't have to say *you idiot.* Her chest cramped as if Geoff's fist had struck its target.

She tapped her boot heel into the ground. "You promised if it stayed in the woods you wouldn't shoot it."

"I did no such thing."

"Maybe it's Mr. Gilbertsen's dog?"

"Old man Gilbertsen was a hunter. He didn't take care of predators. I should have shot that half-breed."

"Then we'd have to fend off all the bears and wolves coming for the carcass. Whatever it is, at least it's not aggressive."

"I don't care. Next time I'm shooting it. I can't afford to lose any more limbs. Or blood."

His last remark hurt more than if that wolf dog had bit through her bone. She gripped the handles of his wheelchair and started pushing him down the trail.

"I've got it," he said.

"No." She pushed his hand away. "Stand watch with the gun."

He turned and gave her a that-isn't-funny glare.

"I'll push. I won't shoot." She steered around a rock embedded in the path.

"Get the basket. You owe me muffins for this bruised face."

"It doesn't look bruised." She leaned over his shoulder to get a closer look at the damage.

"It sure feels bruised." His fingers prodded his cheekbone. "I should demand a refund. How many mistakes is this?" He began counting on his hand. "Three, four…"

"Stop that." She pushed his chair with a little more force to stop his joking. As she retraced their trail, she scanned the forest floor for any movement. The area should have been cleared of game by the gunshot.

Nearing the lodge, she jogged to build up steam and push his chair up the back porch ramp. "You should go lay on the couch. You've been sitting for a while. Flip sides."

He gave a disgruntled sigh and wheeled himself into the living room.

"Do you mind if we eat an early dinner and skip lunch? We'll conserve food that way and do our part for the troops."

"Sure, knock a barrel into my face and starve me. This is why I pay you?" He wheeled into the kitchen and through the dining room. "I need morphine."

"It's early. If I use too much, the count will be off. You said the doctor—"

"I lied." He flashed a satisfied grin. "Doc Miller wants a pain-free patient. Morphine keeps me happy and quiet."

She rubbed the slat of a dining room chair while her mind paged through the instructions she had received her first day on the job. She certainly had enough vials and syringes. Weren't those for an emergency or delay?

"Don't make me butt-sit every one of those steps to your room." He stiff-armed the sofa and lay on the cushions. "If you think I can't get up those stairs to the supply, you're wrong."

"Fine." She could use a restful afternoon. Her bath tumble and wolf encounter had her shaken like a woven rug on a windy day.

She gave him a shot of morphine—against her

better judgment. Peace-filled hours were her reward.

After supper, she sat in the high-backed chair near the couch and worked on needlepoint. With every change of colored thread, she glanced at Geoff who seemed to be memorizing a page in his book.

Lightning flashed.

The bay window behind the couch illuminated like the flicker of a motion picture. Geoff received the best possible reading light.

Oh, no.

Her threaded needle poked through the wrong square.

A drawn-out rumble threatened in the distance.

"Storm's coming." She licked her lips hoping the moisture would stay. Nope. Gone.

He repositioned his left stump. "Great, something else to keep me up at night."

Shushing wind played with the trees.

Bright flash.

Number two.

"I don't like storms." Dropping her needlepoint, she pulled her legs in close to her chest and hugged her knees.

"Judging from the seeding fireweed out back, you only have about six weeks until this rain turns to snow. I'll take the rain."

In. Out. She concentrated on her breathing. In. Not too fast. Out. In.

"Jo?"

The wheelchair parked beside her.

"I'm turning in." The back of his hand brushed her forehead, hesitated, then dropped to the arm rest. "With that inlet out there, it's only going to get worse before it gets better."

She nodded. "I'll check on you before I turn in."

Who was she bluffing? When Geoff fell asleep, she ran upstairs, grabbed the white afghan from her bed, and dashed into his room. What a good plan putting the extra couch near his bed. She wasn't going to sleep alone. Not alone on the second floor.

During the night, she listened to Geoff's occasional groans. The rain's assault on the roof muted some of his grunts.

The thunder retreated down the channel.

Finally.

She snuggled into the afghan, curling into a ball, and into her own personal incubator.

"Over the top. Now. Now. Now!"

She bolted off the couch, arms flailing under white yarn.

Geoff shouted again, less intense, but shrill enough to cause her to panic.

Her heart raced, pounding in her throat as she freed herself from the bedspread. Its warmth fell to her feet.

"Geoff. It's me. We're at the lodge," she said, arms crossed and gripping her shoulders to keep her skeleton in one piece.

He sat up and turned on the light by his bed. "What are you doing in here?" His chest heaved as if he had run a sprint.

"I don't like thunder."

"Then warn me." He gazed around the room. "I thought you were a ghost."

"Ghost? Why would you think I was a ghost?" She picked up the afghan and wrapped it around her shoulders. "You don't believe in them, do you?"

"I usually don't have white blankets dancing

about my room. I almost had a heart attack thinking you were Mr. Gilbertsen."

"He's not here. He's dead."

"Haunted." Geoff's voice was whisper soft, like he was slipping into a dream.

"By our Mr. Gilbertsen? The former owner?" she asked. "I took care of him. He's in glory."

Geoff's head whipped to the side. His lips puckered. A scowl wrinkled his face.

"I can't go on patrol. Not tonight."

She shivered as if thunder had rattled the wall behind her. Geoff acted as if someone else was in the room.

"Tell him, Jo." Geoff's gaze turned to her. "No sentry duty."

No one was there to tell.

"Do it."

Should she talk to the air? She didn't sign up for this—the physical care yes—but the mental? How could she heal someone whose nightmares grew flesh?

"I told you." Geoff held onto every vowel.

Was he talking to her or the man? Wait. No one else existed.

Flinging off the afghan, she balled it up in front of her chest. She could do this. Boss a ghost.

Staring at the closet doors, she cleared her throat and said in her calmest voice, "Please leave. Geoff Chambers is unable to assist you."

There. Done. Then, why was she still looking at the invisible intruder?

Geoff settled into his covers.

She turned to leave, but then she heard a real voice.

"I need more morphine."

And that was the scariest voice of all.

9

She caught the hen coop door before it slammed shut but not before it flattened her middle finger. Her nail bed ridged with white flesh. She held her finger against her tongue to dull the stinging. Tears welled in her eyes. Eyes dry and bloodshot from lack of sleep for four weeks.

Morphine was her enemy. The more morphine Geoff demanded, the more agitated he became, the more nightmares he experienced, the more she wanted to go home. There had to be a way to defeat the enemy.

Heading back to the lodge with her basket of eggs and a throbbing finger, she saw it—the beast. It stood on the path, half-hidden in the fronds of a fern. She froze. Should she call for Geoff? No. One beast to deal with this morning was enough.

She sat on the back porch ramp and waited to see what the wolf dog wanted. It jogged closer, its tail swaying. A round object was visible in its mouth. The animal dropped the object a few yards from where she sat and trotted down the trail.

This animal had to belong to someone—claim jumper, miner, woodsman.

She reached for the object it had dropped and picked up a ripped leather ball.

Ack. The makeshift ball was also soggy.

She threw the toy into the forest.

The beast leapt into the underbrush and emerged with the ball ready for another chase.

"You sure are full of energy on this crisp October morning," she said, tossing the ball down the trail. "But I can't stay and play. Or someone's stomach will be growling with hunger."

She hurried into the kitchen.

"Who were you talking to?" Geoff's question came from the living room.

"Uh." Her heart sped. The tickle of spider's legs crawled up her arms. "Myself."

"If you're that bored, come play cards with me."

She entered the living room. Geoff had pulled the coffee table flush with the couch. He shuffled a deck of cards. More time had been spent rearranging the furniture than on his appearance. Wavy brown hair stuck out like a ruffled collar around his ears. His beard wasn't prickly; it was downright daggers.

"You need a haircut," she said, trying to change the subject. "And breakfast."

"I'll eat and let you cut my hair when you play cards with me. I'm tired of playing alone."

"I don't play cards. My mother says it's a sin." She headed to the kitchen.

"Your stepfather played," he said. "Apparently not well. Afraid you inherited his luck?"

She whipped around. Her hands fisted and sent a sting down her smashed finger. Heat crept across her cheeks. *Offer him candy not vinegar.* Vinegar might be unpredictable, even painful.

Candy won. Almost.

"If my stepfather had listened to my mother and

brought home his paycheck, I wouldn't be here with you."

"Guess I'm the lucky one." He bridge-shuffled the cards.

"Don't speak ill of my stepfather. He worked hard for you out at Kat Wil." Her chest cinched as she spat the name of his precious mine.

He scratched his beard with the two of diamonds. "I shouldn't have said what I did. Guess I'm biased by what Marshal Dorsey told me." He pushed the deck toward her. "Can't we play a silly game of cards?"

Crossing her arms, she stared at her reading chair, not at him.

"Come on, Jo. Didn't you play Pit as a kid? Where's the devil in trading hay and oats?"

Make him happy. Pass the time. Delay the morphine.

"If we burn in hell, I'm going to pester you for eternity." She sat at the coffee table. "And don't think I've forgotten about cutting that rodent's nest hair of yours."

Her fingers drummed on the table.

"What are we playing?"

"Gin Rummy," he said, starting to deal.

"You must like it hot."

He laughed, deep and long, like a car backfiring.

"Rummy's simple," he said. "Collect three or four of a number or make a run, such as the nine, ten, and Jack. All of the same suit. Diamonds. Hearts. Clubs. Spades." He threw out cards to illustrate his point. "Now, for the numbers." He rifled through the deck and found sixes. "They'll be different suits. Aces are low. They're ones. First one to one-hundred wins. If you're ready to go out, knock on the table."

"You don't expect me to understand all that, do

you?"

"I'll coach you. It's not like we're pressed for time."

"Let's get one thing straight before we begin," she said. "I'm not betting. I'm expecting some birthday money to arrive when Tubby comes again, and I'll be darned if I'm losing it to you." She clasped her hand over her mouth.

"Josephine Nimetz. Did I hear a near curse word come from your mouth?" A mischievous grin enlivened his haggard face. "When's the big day?"

"October twenty-sixth. I'll be eighteen."

He cut the deck into two small piles. "Three days, hmm? For me, eighteen seems like a century ago."

"You're not that old. Are you?" She tugged at her skirt, wondering if she had offended him. Her mother said never to discuss age.

"I sure feel old. I'll be twenty-one on Christmas Eve."

"Then I'll be sure to make you a big chocolate cake."

"I don't like chocolate."

"I've never met anyone who doesn't like chocolate. What do you prefer?"

"Strawberry."

"Well, on my birthday it's going to be chocolate. You're out of luck. Now deal."

They each received ten cards. She organized her hand by numbers and suits. Nah. It couldn't be. She had a court of royals. Pretending to be watching the hens roost, she picked a card from the pile and knocked on the table and discarded.

"You can't be serious," he said. "What do you have, Runt?"

She laid her hand down. "A run. I think. King, Queen, Jack, ten, all hearts, and four eights. Only two aces left in my hand and they're ones. Right?" Her stomach felt like it was popping corn. "Can you beat it?"

"No," he said, leaning back on the couch. "I must not have shuffled well enough."

"Or my luck isn't cursed?"

"And mine is?"

"How many points is that?" she asked, not wanting to dwell on sinner's luck.

He figured the difference between their hands.

"Ninety-eight points."

"This shouldn't take long if I need a hundred to win."

He handled the deck for an extra long time, shuffling, bridging, shuffling, bridging. He threw ten cards her way.

This hand lasted longer. He knocked on the table with a satisfied smirk.

Placing her cards on the table, she laid down four twos and played three cards on his runs. Counting the cards in their hands, she had one less in her total than he.

"Do I get any points for that?" She pressed her lips together and waited for him to declare her the winner.

"Yes, you're over 100." His eyes pinched shut. He rubbed his forehead as if he was tallying scores in his brain.

"I'd better start the stove." She rose from the table.

"I want a re-match. And a shot."

Not this early. But she climbed the stairs to her room, to the metal morphine box, to a reprimand from somebody—Doctor Miller, Mrs. Prescott, Mr.

Chambers—what would overdosing for ten months do to Geoff's health? Would he survive? Could she survive without the tranquility it gave her patient?

He had to be lying. Someone was keeping track of the narcotics.

She heard him tapping the deck on the table like an impatient child.

Filling the syringe, an idea came to her. It came from the cards. She didn't need to fill the syringe with a King, Queen, and Jack. A simple three sevens would be enough. Geoff didn't inspect the dosage when she gave him a shot. He looked away and waited for the poke. By the time Tubby came again, Geoff's dosage would be back to pre-lodge levels.

The *thunk* of the card deck grew louder.

"Jo, I need that shot."

She closed the metal box and hurried downstairs.

Perhaps playing Gin Rummy wasn't so sinful. Perhaps her morphine dosing plan would work. Perhaps it wouldn't have been bad to place a token bet. She erased the thought from her mind. All she could see was the image of her stepfather's body slumped in the woods—slain.

10

"Watch it with those scissors. I don't want to lose any more body parts."

She straightened Geoff's hair between her fingers and trimmed the split ends. Water trickled down her arm. At least the sensation helped keep her awake and alert.

"The blades will rust with all this water. Didn't you dry your hair?" She grabbed a dish towel from the kitchen counter and rubbed it across his head. The fresh scent of his shampoo hung in the air.

His head bobbed as she massaged his scalp. She moved her hands in a circular motion down to his neck.

Groaning, he lifted his head and stared at the ceiling. "I'm in pain. I need relief."

Stall.

Her stomach muscles clenched, cinching her waist smaller than a dressmaker's dummy. "It's too early. It's only been a few hours since your shot at breakfast. How about more cards when I'm through?"

He grasped her arm, pulling her over the back of his chair. Scissors protruded from her hand.

She didn't want to be this close. She tensed. Her eyes slammed shut. Her lips melted together like creamed butter on fresh baked biscuits.

"I have a need. You're supposed to meet my needs. Now, follow my orders and give me a shot."

His grip tightened and tightened and tightened some more.

She nodded in agreement.

"I'll take these," he said, removing the scissors from her tingling hand, freeing her to get the narcotic.

She didn't leave.

"I want my scissors," she said, grabbing his chair. "No scissors, no morphine. I'll break one rule, but I won't break them all." Her cheekbones could boil broth.

"Here." He held out the scissors, blades open. "Take 'em."

"Close the blades, Mr. Chambers."

She waited.

He snapped the blades shut and handed her the scissors. His arm trembled terribly.

"My shot." His voice crackled like a low burning fire.

She drew a third of the customary dose of morphine, the amount she had given him earlier in the day, after cards. She stood by her decision to give him what he received in Juneau. After the injection, while disposing of the needle, she heard him shout, "I'm shuffling."

After more cards playing, she cooked and cleaned until evening. Geoff insisted on dining in his room to escape her clattering and clanking.

Her day's labor done, she settled into her reading chair with *Woman's Home Companion.*

The romantic serials left her wondering what would happen next. Subscribers had to wait a whole month to find out if there was going to be a wedding or a scandal. It seemed cruel to keep readers in suspense, but the editors knew what they were doing—printing money. Fortunately, she didn't have to wait a whole month to find out the ending to the storyline. Mrs. Prescott had sent the August and September issues along with her to the lodge.

The women in the stories, sketched to look like movie actresses, kept her spellbound. Wavy hair primped perfectly, complimented the stylish fashions. An illustrated breeze swept form-fitting crepe de chine dresses away from curvy bodies. Handsome love interests, perfectly suited in style and wealth, came to call on the women, strong in build, yet vulnerable with desire.

She became the woman in the story, embraced by the broad shoulders of an attractive suitor, imagining how it would feel to kiss his lips as he held her close to his firm chest.

"What are you reading?"

Her body twitched—all at once—sending her heart into a spasm. Lost in the world of *Woman's Home Companion*, she had not heard Geoff enter the room. She shut the magazine, keeping her thumb in the serial.

"You startled me."

"Is the story any good? What's it about?" He wheeled closer to her chair.

"Women's things," she answered. "Sewing. Baking. You wouldn't be interested in the newest wood polish." She fanned herself with the magazine trying to calm down after her start.

He studied her face as if he was determining whether she had a winning hand at cards. "Wood polish, eh? It must be quite a product to make your cheeks that red. I even heard a giggle when I entered the room."

"You scared me. It's no wonder I'm flushed."

He held his hand out for the magazine.

She stopped fanning and tried to pull her page-marking thumb out of the *Companion*. "I'm not finished."

He was too quick. Seizing her wrist with one hand, he confiscated the magazine with the other.

"Not finished with what? Advertisements?"

"Give it back." Her words deflated in defeat.

He wheeled toward the hearth and turned to face her. He flipped through the pages and began reading.

She glared at him while her boot tap, tap tapped against the floor.

"These two people really like one another. Don't they? I can see why you were blushing. This gentleman's a sweet talker. Don't you think?"

She shifted, facing the side of the chair, her back a shield from his inquisition.

"I don't know. I'm tired." Her jaw muscles tightened. "I don't know him."

"There must be something about him that keeps you reading. Tell me one thing and I'll give this back to you." He wheeled closer and dangled the *Companion* in front of her.

She blew out a disgruntled breath.

"He has big shoulders."

"And?"

"Muscular arms."

"How can you tell that?" He inspected the drawing. "The man's wearing a suit."

Rising to her feet, she reached for the magazine. "You said if I told you one thing you'd give it back."

"You told me two." He belly laughed and rolled backward, taunting her with the *Companion*. "Besides, I paid for this, and I won't pay for you to sit there lusting over a drawing of a phony man. Especially, when I need pain relief."

No morphine. Not for a few more hours.

"I wasn't lusting. I was reading." She cinched her hands at her waist and stomped one last time—hard. "Now, give it back."

"Sure. Pay me. It's only twenty cents."

Her anger charred her insides. She had no money. Her mother depended on her earnings and he knew it. She envisioned screaming into his stubbly face and pummeling his body with her fists.

"I might want to read this story myself," he continued. "This woman's drawn very well. Rather pretty wouldn't you say?"

Josephine's face flushed. She could be dolled up pretty if Geoff didn't drain all her energy. Working all night and all day had to stop. She had to stop the morphine. Stop the erratic behavior. Stop the nightmares.

I won't make it until June. Not with the drugs. I'll fail. For me and my family.

She bolted up the stairs and removed aspirin and syringes and ointments from the medicine box. Carrying the box close to her chest, she raced downstairs. There would be no more abuse of the doctor's orders. No more abuse of her dignity.

The front door was in reach.

"What do you have there?" His voice rose, questioning, but like he already knew the answer.

She opened the door.

Frigid night air blasted her face.

One staggered breath. Two.

She jogged down the steps.

"What are you doing?" His wheels *whirred* on the porch. "Get back here. Obey me!"

At full stride, she hit the dock. Glass vials jostled and clinked with her movements. Reaching the end of the wooden bridge, she whipped out the vials. Fistfuls of morphine bottles flew into the inlet. The midnight-blue water sucked the drug into its depths.

Done.

There was nothing she could do to bring the morphine back.

Bending over, her mouth blew puffs of smoke into the moonlit air as if she were a small steam engine. Her heart chased her lungs trying to keep a pace, keep rhythm. The burning in her throat flashed down her windpipe.

When her panting subsided, she turned and faced the lodge.

His wheelchair blocked the front doorway.

"Look at me," she called out, raising her arms for all of nature to take notice. "I cannot be that woman in the magazine. I have lost weight. My skin is dry as dust. My hair is duller than this life."

Tripping on a stone at the edge of the dock, she fell to her knees. Frost dampened her dress. "Take it," she shouted, rubbing mud from her palms. "Take the magazine. Why should I read about other people's happiness? Keep your twenty cents." The wet ground under her knees felt like rock bottom.

The light from the doorway started to vanish.

Fear-drenched adrenaline fired up her heart.

"No," she cried, stumbling toward the porch steps. She was almost at the door. So close. Close enough to hear the lock shift into place.

11

She had to get inside the lodge. The cold had kept its distance while she was running down to the dock but now it nipped at her skin and seeped into her bones.

"Geoff." She pounded on the front door.

No answer.

The blood pulsing through her veins echoed in her head as if her skull had turned hollow.

Think.

Rounding the lodge at full speed, she scaled the ramp to the kitchen door. With a twist of the doorknob, she shouldered the door and prayed it would open.

No luck.

Geoff's shadow was visible through the curtains.

"Please, Geoff. Let me in."

She knocked until the side of her fist split open and blood settled into the cracks of her skin.

Her back bumped against the horizontal logs of the lodge as she dropped to a sitting position. She had no coat to keep her warm, no gloves, not even a hat. She never thought Geoff would lock her out of the lodge. Yell. Pinch. Curse. Yes. But lock her out where she could die?

Chunks of glacier ice seemed to clog the

circulation to her toes and fingers. She rubbed her hands together and crunched her toes to melt the blood slush.

Out of the corner of her eye, she saw ferns swaying in the underbrush. *Bear? Wolf? Moose?*

She eased out her breaths—long, quiet, and controlled.

An animal emerged from the black timbers. Its back end wiggled.

Whistling or calling the beast wasn't an option. Her lips couldn't pucker. She clapped once. The vibration stung her hands.

The beast jogged up the ramp, slowed, then sat by her side. She welcomed his warm breath and thick fur. Stroking his winter coat gave her fingers life. But then she remembered the gun. What if Geoff heard the clack of the beast's paws on the porch? Would he shoot her friend? Her back stiffened. What if Geoff did something to harm himself? Would the marshal hold her responsible? Even if the law didn't blame her, she would hold herself responsible.

"I've got to check on Geoff."

The dog quirked his head at her statement.

Glancing around the yard, she spied the wood pile. She ran and grabbed a log, juggling the ice-glazed wood in her hands. She threw the log into the glass of the back door. The pane shattered. Glass shards fell onto the kitchen floor. Careful not to bloody her hand, she reached in and found the key in the lock. Her breathy exhale fogged the air. Success.

Wide-eyed, she rushed into the lodge, welcoming the warmth from the kerosene heaters.

Geoff was spread out on the bed, facing the ceiling, no covers on his body. His shirt lay on the floor. His skin had an unusual gleam as if he had been misted with water. He reached for her when she entered the room.

"I need my morphine." His gaze stayed fixed on the ceiling. "And I need you to rub my feet." His muscles tensed, making his body as rigid as the plank she had tossed through the window.

What have I done?

Tears tingled behind her eyes. "I threw the morphine in the inlet." Her voice rasped from the cold.

His eyes dilated like a startled barn owl. "I thought that was a dream?"

"Now, I wish it was. Chalk up another mistake." She struggled to remove his pants. Pushing her palms into where the surgeons had sealed up his stumps, she caressed his scars. His skin was too warm. Her fingers weren't warm enough.

Short bursts of sound exited his mouth. Not screams. More like groans with intense fluctuations.

"I'm sorry." Her throat seized as she stared at his strained face. "I thought it would get easier without the drugs. They made things difficult." *They made it difficult for me.*

His body quaked.

"I tried to do what the doctor said. You wouldn't listen." Her voice cracked with fear. Fear short of panic. This wasn't pneumonia. The doctor wasn't a phone call away. "I'll do a better job. Tell me what to do."

"Stay with me," he said before his teeth clamped shut.

She stayed. Dutifully, massaging his limbs and wiping the sweat from his face. When the thrashing started, she retreated to the couch in his room, but not before laying pillows on the floor by his bed.

Geoff bolted into a sitting position.

"Danny. Barbed wire. Entrench."

He was going where she could not follow. Where she didn't want to follow.

Geoff eased back into the covers—mumbling—most likely to Danny.

When he quieted, she laid on the bed next to him.

"Jo?"

Her eyes shot open.

"I'm burning."

"I'll get the aspirin." She scrambled to her feet.

"Water. Lots of water."

She hurried to the kitchen and filled a pitcher with cold water. She remembered bringing him water from the expensive crystal pitcher at the mansion. One month with her, and he looked worse than the night they had met.

He drank two glasses of water and sank back into bed.

She reached out to stroke his legs.

"Don't touch my legs." His warning came fast and sharp like an arrow. "My skin's on fire."

She felt his forehead. No fever. When he fell back to sleep, she slept.

Late morning, she strapped on a work apron and scurried off to feed the chickens and load up on wood. She set bread to rise using white flour, skipping the addition of other grains for "war bread." No one could question her sacrifice for the doughboys. She set tea to steep.

Laughter rang out from the living room. "Got you, you louse."

She rushed to the living room. What else did Geoff

have to endure? What else did she?

Her heartbeat thrummed in her ears. "Geoff?"

He didn't acknowledge her. He sat on the couch with a lit candle in his hand. The flame almost scorched his bare stomach. He lifted the fire closer to his neck, his chin, his hair. One twitch and he would be ablaze.

"I got another one, Danny. I'll get rid of them once and for all. Dreaded lice."

She inched toward the couch and tried not to startle Geoff. Why did he have to have these nightmares? Taking care of him was hard enough without the ghosts.

The candle moved up the center of his chest, around what looked like an imaginary collar, down his left arm, and circled his wrist. If he dropped the candle, she was sure the rug would ignite.

"Let me help you." Her voice was calm, almost upbeat like this was a mundane chore. But inwardly, she was aware of every motion her body made, every swallow, every exhale.

She reached for the candle.

Geoff flinched.

The candle slipped between his fingers. He jerked causing the candle to drop to the ground.

The carpet smoldered. A toasted yarn scent filled the room.

She stomped on the carpet and trampled the start of a flame. Bending over to see if the fire had gone out, a canister of tea fell from her apron pocket.

"Mustard gas." Geoff lunged forward. His clammy chest slammed into hers.

Air whooshed from her lungs. Their bodies missed shattering the coffee table. Her shoulder rammed the front of her reading chair. Pain radiated down her arm. She lay on the floor as starbursts blurred her vision. Geoff's half-naked body pinned her against the pine planks.

"Move," she gasped.

His body relaxed, but it did not move. She feared waking him. What if he viewed her as the enemy? A German spy? Getting tackled again or having to fight a frightened soldier would be dangerous.

She laid still. Her heart and lungs pumped like steam engines on an uphill climb. His shallow breaths tickled her neck. Closing her eyes, she pretended she was playing a part in a movie. Everything was make-believe. Nothing was real. She had played this game before when her parents fought and Ivan had won.

What time was it? She couldn't see the clock. Had an hour passed? Minutes? She thought about the tea steeping in the kitchen. It was probably cold by now. How she wished she had drank some before trying to disarm Geoff.

Finally, Geoff shifted. He rolled toward the table. His eyes opened slowly and grew wide. Wider when he saw her.

"Are you all right? Did I hurt you?"

His eyes filled with disbelief at her sprawled-out frame. He studied her face as if he was looking for a scratch, or a bruise, or blood. His head bobbed like a hungry hen at feeding time as he surveyed their surroundings.

"What happened?"

She took hold of his arm and pulled herself up. "Nothing. You've done nothing. Except try to save me from mustard gas."

"Gas?" He dragged himself to the couch and used

it as a back rest. "I must have been at the front."

She stretched her hands to the ceiling. "You called out to a man. A man named Danny."

"Danny O'Rourke."

"You've mentioned him before. Was he a friend?" She sat next to him on the floor.

Geoff stared at the fire—its waning embers barely visible through the ash logs.

"He was my trench mate. He died in the explosion that took my legs. Saved my life."

"How's that possible?" She rubbed her arms. Without Geoff's body for warmth, her skin chilled.

"Danny fell across my body. His weight slowed the bleeding from my limbs." Geoff's shoulders slumped as his head rested against the couch cushion. "We used to tease him about his weight. Only guy we knew who gained pounds in France."

"I'm so sorry." Everything about the war seemed to bring him grief. "I shouldn't have asked."

His torso shivered.

"Let's get you back to bed."

"No, I want to stay out here by the fire."

She struggled to stand. Her joints needed an oil can.

"Where are you going?"

"To get you a blanket and…um…and to pee." She untied her apron.

He glanced down at his pants. "Guess I already did."

"It's a thick apron. Washable." She turned to leave. "I'll get you some fresh clothes."

"What day is it?" He rubbed his forehead as if he summoned memories from the past two days.

"It's Friday. Tomorrow is my birthday." She

steadied herself against his bedroom door.

He gazed upon her with eyes as lifeless as the ashen logs. "Here's my present. When Tubby comes, get on the *Maiden*. Leave me the new morphine." His eyes slammed shut. "On the couch, leave the rifle."

12

She whirled around. Her ears hummed. Her fists curled. Her face flushed as if she had checked the oven's temperature for supper. How could he even suggest she leave after all she had done for him? Leave him to a no-good end. She couldn't go home a failure. What would Mr. Chambers think? Her mother? Ann?

"Are you firing me?" She choked out her words between dry sobs. "Because I'm not leaving. I'm a good nurse." She stomped her foot. "I am." *And good nurses don't leave weapons with hurting people.*

"Go lay down, Jo. You look worse than I feel."

"I will not." She stomped over to the hearth and threw a log on the fire. Then another.

Stepping back from the hearth, she jabbed a finger at the rifle on the wall. "And that...that..." She couldn't bring herself to name the weapon. "Is for protection. Nothing else." Her arm shook so violently she brought it to her side. "Look around you, Geoff Chambers. Look around you." Her voice grew too loud for the living room. "Count your blessings. I have never lived in a place this nice."

He stared at her as if she were a stranger sauntering into the lodge.

She grabbed a cup off the coffee table and wished

it were something larger she could hide behind. She glanced in his direction. "Captain Barrie will be stopping by in the next few days. I don't want him to see this mess. If I don't strip your bed and wash your soiled clothes, he won't come near the door."

"Oh, he'll come. And if he finds out I blacked out and left you in the cold—" Geoff leaned forward and punched the table for emphasis. "The reason Tubby stops here is to see if you're all right. For all he cares, I could be stone cold dead."

"Don't say such a thing. I'm not going to let you die."

"How many times have you almost killed me?"

She stilled. Pressure mounted behind her eyes liked a kinked hose. She pressed the cup into her belly to keep her muscles from cramping and plopped into her reading chair. The high back cushions seemed to be the only support she had at the moment. The newly invigorated embers of the fire held her attention. "I didn't know what I was doing throwing the morphine away. I didn't realize it would be so bad. I've never done this before. Taken care of someone with such..."

"Such what?"

"Need," she said, her tears flowing freely. "I'm doing the best I can. I guess I should have stuck to sewing." Her fingers quivered as she swiped a tear from her cheek.

"Hey." He dragged his body over to where she sat and tugged at her skirt. "I'm alive. Forget about the mistakes. I shouldn't have run off at the mouth."

She shook her head. "We can do better." Ragged breaths shook her chest. "We have to do better."

"And we will." His pity-filled eyes and lopsided grin didn't overflow with confidence.

Her stomach growled in agreement. "Are you hungry?"

"I could use some tea." He let go of her skirt.

"What a coincidence." She blotted her cheeks. "So could I."

~*~

That night, she checked in on Geoff before she headed up to her room to change into a nightgown. He lay in bed facing the doorway, wide awake, his newly cropped hair still damp from his bath.

Crossing her arms, she leaned against the doorframe. "Are you in pain?"

"No, I don't think I am."

"Good."

"I just can't seem to fall asleep." He propped himself up with his elbow. "How 'bout a game of rummy?"

"At this hour?"

He opened the drawer of his nightstand and pulled out a deck of cards. "Just one?"

She sighed and perched on the edge of his bed. Arguing was futile. He always got his way. Well, almost always.

"Thank you." He shuffled the deck.

"For what? Beating you at cards?"

"For being a headstrong runt, and running off with my morphine."

"You're most welcome. I'll take that as a compliment." She cocked her head and hid her smug smile. Her bold action had worked out for the best. For both of them. "Now deal."

~*~

Josephine woke to shouts booming outside the lodge. Why was she not in her bed? Why was she in Geoff's? Splayed on the bed sheet in front of her was a decent hand of cards. Geoff was asleep, resting against a mound of pillows half as high as the headboard. If he had legs, his toes would be tickling her nostrils. She must have fallen asleep.

Oh no! She leapt to her feet. *Tubby.* What would the captain think if he found her in Geoff's bedroom with the lodge a mess?

"Geoff. Wake up." She shook his longest stump. "Tubby's here."

"So," he mumbled, not even bothering to open his eyes.

She ironed her wrinkled gingham dress with her hand. "I'm a mess. The lodge is a mess."

"Tubby won't mind."

"I mind." She raced into the living room to pick up blankets and dishes and tea cups.

Tubby knocked. "Jo?" he bellowed.

Too late.

She folded Geoff's blanket and used it to shield her disheveled dress. Plastering a good morning grin on her face, she opened the door.

"Happy Bir—" Tubby's pipe sagged. "What the heck happened to you?" He brushed by her and bent over, half-sliding, half-kicking a box next to the couch.

"Uh… Geoff's been ill." Her heart bounced like a paddleball under the captain's inquisitive stare. It wasn't a lie. She didn't have to admit her mistake. "I haven't slept."

"Not the influenza, is it?" Tubby marched outside and picked up a pink box from the porch.

"I don't think so. There's no fever."

"Good. That sickness almost caught us in Nome. Wherever it goes it leaves a graveyard." Tubby stepped into the lodge and handed her the small box. "Chocolate cake. From your mother. Now close that door before a gust blows you clear out the back of this lodge."

She offered Tubby tea and cake. He accepted both.

"I've got letters and cards for you," Tubby said, wiping frosting from his whiskers. "That big box is full of business ledgers and papers for Master Chambers. "Your mother packed up a crate of sewing what-nots, too."

Not wanting to waste any of her birthday cake, she smashed the last remaining crumbs with her fork. "Organizing the threads will give me something fun to do today."

"I would have been here sooner." Tubby shook his head. "With the troubles in Nome, I got detained on a trip for Mr. Todd."

"Brice Todd?"

"His father." The captain cocked his head. "You know the family?"

"Not really. I met Brice at the Chamberses' house before we left for the lodge." The mention of Brice's name left a sour citrus taste in her mouth.

"Should have guessed he'd be there. Those two boys go back a long way. I used to ferry them and their friends on my boat." Tubby rubbed his whiskers as he reminisced. "They sure knew how to have fun. It's a shame about the war." He nodded toward the bedroom door.

Josephine didn't want to pry, but she was curious about a certain friend mentioned at the mansion.

She placed Tubby's dirty plate on top of her dish.

"Do you remember a friend of theirs—a girl named Christine?"

"Christine Reid? Tall, fair-haired, kind of shy?"

Her cake settled like a stone in her stomach. Christine was her opposite. Oh, why should she care? "I think so."

"She been out here?" Tubby leaned closer as if for a piece of seafaring gossip.

"No." She rose and stacked the dishes. "Geoff mentioned her. At the mansion." Or was it Brice?

Tubby's gaze swept the room. "Is he treating you well?" His voice barely crossed the table.

She nodded and brushed a few wayward crumbs into her hand. No need to go into the details of the last few weeks. The weeks ahead could only get better.

"Geoff's manageable. I'm tired and a little homesick, that's all."

Tubby re-lit his pipe. Fire sparked off the tobacco as he puffed into the stem. The aroma of baked apples and ash filled the dining room.

"I'd like to stay longer, but I've got to get the *Maiden* up to Skagway." He stood and patted her shoulder. "It's good we had our visit."

Saved by a schedule. She was too tired to answer an inquisition from Tubby.

"Thank you for bringing the gifts and supplies." She accompanied him to the door and opened it.

"After November, I may not get back this way for a while. Mother Nature's got a lot to do with that. There's a musher out this way that can bring the mail." Tubby turned and blew a ring of smoke into the cool morning. The lazy O disintegrated over the porch misting a smoky fruit scent into the air. He bent over and picked up a metal box. The old, empty medicine box.

A shiver washed over her skin, whip-starting her heart. *He knew they were out of morphine.* She licked her lips tasting a hint of cocoa and sugar.

Tubby held up his find. The lid flopped open displaying a few damp cotton balls and a tube of spent ointment. "Since I discovered this container at the end of the dock, I'm assuming you have Geoff's pain under control."

She cleared her throat and tried to make the jumbled confession in her head into a coherent sentence. "Please take any new morphine back to Dr. Miller." Placing a hand on his arm, she said, "We're as good as gold."

"Hah. Fool's gold discarded in a creek maybe."

Her posture stiffened at his assessment. "I'm not a fool."

Tubby's gaze did not leave hers for what seemed like a million seconds. "Never thought you were." He latched the box. "If Chambers ever hurts you, I'll get here and take you back to Juneau, no questions asked. Just like I didn't ask about that boarded-up back window."

Her mouth fell open. She shut it fast. "Thank you, Tubby. I'm doing my best."

"Of that," the captain said through pipe puckered lips, "I have no doubts."

She waved to Tubby one last time as he boarded the *Maiden.*

When the door was firmly closed, Geoff wheeled into the living room.

"You could have gone."

"And leave you with this mess?" She shook her head. "But I do hope Tubby brought material for a new bedspread. I don't think I'll get the stains out of your old one."

"It doesn't matter. I've slept in worse." Geoff lifted the flaps on the cardboard box Tubby had placed near the couch. "This mine business should keep me out of your hair. Except for this." He held out a magazine. October's *Companion.*

Memories of their argument flooded into her brain.

"Take it." He rustled the pages. "There might be advertisements for a new polish or cleanser. Your red cheeks will tell me when you're reading the story about the big man."

Guilt pinged her chest. She shouldn't have mentioned the handsome and healthy men in the serials. She took the magazine from him. "Speaking of that man—"

"I wasn't."

She met his bloodshot gaze. "Would you like breakfast?"

"Yes, but not chocolate cake."

"More for me then." She spun on her heels. "Eggs for you."

Hunger was a good sign. A sign she had made the right decision by discarding the morphine and staying at the lodge.

Her decision was definitely not a mistake.

Happy eighteenth birthday to me!

13

After Geoff ate breakfast, she gathered her cards and letters and headed up to her room, her sanctuary. Her mother's letter concerned her. The last few sentences, written in Ann's elegant handwriting, contrasted greatly with her mother's unsteady cursive. The new arthritis treatment was a failure. But then, it had only been a month since she had left Juneau to take care of Geoff. Now that her mother had a steady income, she could try another remedy.

Ann's own letter described the men she had met recently in town. More miners, a salesman, and another poor soul Josephine was too busy to care about.

As she sat reading, she heard a strange puffing sound coming from downstairs. Pressing her ear to the door, she listened intently, trying to make out what Geoff was doing. Finally, she headed downstairs to make sure he didn't hurt himself.

In the corner of the living room, she saw him, stretched out and facing the floor. His torso moved up and down. When his chest lifted off the floor, he exhaled, sounding like a storm wind.

"What are you doing?" she asked.

No answer.

Was he upset with her? *Oh, why did I have to mention anything about men's biceps?* She watched him pump up and down. "This isn't about that serial in the magazine. Is it?"

He froze at the height of a push-up and flipped himself over.

"I stormed up hills with a heavy pack on my back, carried barbed wire, bandoliers of ammunition, and a bayonet at the ready. I stayed alive. Don't you ever compare me to some imaginary gent sketched in a woman's magazine."

Her pulse quickened. His combative reply reminded her of Ivan's outbursts. Punishment usually accompanied her stepfather's rage. Childhood tricks flashed into her brain. Hide. Run. Apologize.

"I didn't mean to..." She hugged her waist and glanced at the sheen on the coffee table.

Geoff turned over and continued his routine. Up. Down. Up. Down.

She'd leave him be. Since Geoff was preoccupied, she decided to clean his bedroom. While she sorted his closet, she would look for a place to store his old bedspread. The sooner he had a new bed covering, the sooner they could put the memory of his withdrawal behind them.

The box of mining papers Tubby had brought to the lodge took up space on the closet floor, not to mention Geoff had a complete wardrobe of pants, long, short and uneven. She scanned the room for another storage site for the box. The small closet, half-hidden by the lamp on the nightstand on the other side of the bed, caught her attention. That door hadn't been disturbed since they moved into the lodge.

After removing clutter, she braced her hand on the

closet frame and jimmied the warped door open. A large rectangular box leaned across the bottom of the closet. Empty shelving occupied the rest. Good. Lots of storage.

She bent over and picked up the box—a box with considerable weight. Had the lone box belonged to Mr. Gilbertsen? Maybe Mrs. Gilbertsen didn't even know it existed. For sure, the widow would want its contents. Something shifted inside. Placing her find on the bed, she cut the twine securing the flaps with Geoff's nail scissors. Upon opening, she spied two long tubes wrapped in linen. When she picked up the first tube, her grip slipped, and a black dress shoe emerged from the cloth.

A man's shoe.

Her fingers trembled as she pushed the linen over the shiny black leather and up a wooden replica of a leg.

She knew it wasn't real but she dropped the fake appendage on the bed as if it were infected with the influenza. White broadcloth straps unfurled above the fake knee.

"Geoff, can you come into the bedroom?" She kept her tone free of accusation, but who else did she know who needed wooden feet?

"In a minute." Geoff blew out a loud breath as if his last push up was worth a prize.

Soon, she heard his wheels crossing the living room floor. When he entered his room, he halted near the French doors.

"What is this?" She held up the leg and tried to untangle the attached straps.

"Watch it. Those straps are impossible to straighten out."

She pointed the black shoe in his direction. "How long have you had these? You've never mentioned having wooden legs."

"I've had them since the hospital." He repositioned himself in his chair.

And kept them a secret. "Won't your father expect to see you wearing them come June?"

"It's not my father's business if I wear them or not. They hurt. And it takes too much effort to move around in those logs."

She could sense a battle coming. Speaking as if to sell the latest and most expensive fashions, she said, "But your bed sores are much better. What if we could get them totally healed. Now, that you're weaned from the morphine—"

"Weaned?" He furrowed his forehead.

"Your phantom pains might lessen with exercise." She laid the leg back on the bed. "I think we should try these. Don't you want to look normal?"

His face stilled as if he sensed an enemy nearby. "The Germans took care of that."

She wished she could gulp back her words. Her lips went dry. Moisture seeped into her palms. "I want your father to think I've done a good job. If he expects you to be walking—"

"He doesn't. Your job is to keep me alive and out of his wife's hair. You're doing that. I'm more alive now than when I was in his house. Although, he lets me win at cards once in a while."

"Don't mention the cards," she snapped. "My mother would have a fit if she found out I was playing rummy."

"So, I shouldn't mention cards." He folded his hands in his lap. "What else? Splitting bedsores, hurling my medication in the inlet, slapping me?"

"We're forgetting about my mistakes. Remember?" Her temples throbbed a warning not to anger him.

"Sew me a new bedspread. Whatever you want. You don't have to worry about the legs."

Her foot tapped an annoyed rhythm while she batted her eyes at the wooden planks above her.

"Besides," he continued, "even if I did become proficient at walking with them, I'd need a new wardrobe. You'd have to hide straps and flare pant legs."

"Done." She relaxed her neck and beheld his slack-jawed face. "You said I could sew whatever I want."

He started to back track his chair out of the room. "I didn't agree to use the legs."

"But if I made you slacks to fit the legs, you'd have something to practice in." She controlled her smile so it didn't seem as though she was gloating.

He turned an about-face and shoved off toward the living room. "I can't win. It's a gift you have, supernatural or otherwise, that lets you win ninety-nine percent of the time. Measure me at your own peril. But only after my nap." He stopped and glanced back. "I warn you, those straps are hec—."

"Horrible." She corrected him. "Those straps are horrible."

He grinned as if he figured out the punch line to a joke. "At least we agree."

~*~

"Hand me my right leg." Geoff gestured to the shorter wooden limb composed of a shoe, calf and knee. He sat on the bed wearing a long-sleeve white shirt that snapped down to his crotch and formed underwear. "The German's didn't blow off as much of my right one."

She picked up the prosthetic leg. It shone brownish-black except for an egg shell colored kneecap. Wide straps that hooked below the knee dragged on the floor. Her stomach hollowed as she envisioned joining the wood to his stump.

"You'll have to push as I pull it on." He took the limb from her and lined it up with his stump.

Trying not to stare at his puckered flesh, she gave a gentle push. His leg sank two inches into the wood.

"The straps fasten up here on my chest." He secured the buckles.

The left leg, much longer than the right, was more difficult to attach. She poked skin into the opening with her fingers as he eased the indentation over the end of his upper thigh. She anchored the straps from the top of his leg, over his shoulder, and across his chest.

"We'll need to tighten the straps when I stand up." He grabbed the bedpost and drew to a height over six-feet tall. He towered over her.

A maze of straps and buckles crisscrossed his torso. Designing a shirt that would hide everything was going to be difficult. Flaring his pant legs was the least of her concerns. Aligning a pant zipper with the unitard underneath would be more of a challenge. The wheelchair looked better every minute.

She wrapped the tape measure around his chest. His body twitched.

"Ticklish?" she asked.

"No." His voice trembled. "But you're more of a

runt from up here."

Hopping on the bed, she said, "Hold out your arms." With the bed underfoot, she was not a runt anymore. When she was done measuring, she poked him in the ribs with her finger.

"Watch it. Sudden movements make me fall."

"Inseam next." She stepped down and knelt in front of him. A rush of heat warmed her cheeks as her hand hovered above his inner thigh.

He cleared his throat. "I'll hold the top of the tape."

"I usually do dresses."

"That might be a solution."

"Your father would not be amused." She tilted forward as she stood.

"Don't lean into me." His eyes bulged as if in fright. He tried to steady himself. "Move." He pushed her away as he teetered.

Losing his balance, he careened backward. She jumped to the side but not soon enough.

Crack.

A dull, throbbing ache shot across her face from her chin to her cheek. Salty, tin-tasting blood teased her tongue. A wave rolled through her stomach. She pressed her palm against her jaw as if to hold it in place. How would she explain being decked by a fake shoe?

Reaching forward, Geoff tried to peel her fingers off her jawbone. "Can you move your mouth? Good heavens, say something."

"Unfortunately for you." She sounded like a toothless old seaman. "Nothing's broken. I'll be fine. I might need to borrow some of your aspirin."

Geoff helped her to her feet.

"Lay on the bed. I'll get a wet cloth." He waddled to the bathroom, arms straight in front, as if he were blind and expected to crash into a wall. Her gaze followed his strange, calculated gait. She had never seen him walk except on his stumps, but this was a normal-height walk. He definitely was over six-feet tall.

He returned and handed her a cool cloth. "I'll get you something to read. Just rest."

The compress silenced the drum beat that seemed to be reverberating through her jawbone.

Tottering back into the bedroom, Geoff handed her *Woman's Home Companion*.

She stared into his gray eyes and grinned. "My injury must be worse than it feels."

He laughed. Geoff Chambers actually laughed. For her, that was better medicine than an aspirin.

14

With every tick of the clock, Geoff came to check on her injury. He wheeled into the bedroom, without his wooden legs, and perched his chair next to the nightstand.

"I'll have your pants by tomorrow." She needed to get back to work.

"Let it go. Isn't a bruised jaw enough for you?"

"Apparently not." She shifted to the edge of his bed and sat. She didn't know how to tell him that seeing him walking gave her satisfaction. Satisfaction in her decision to stay. Satisfaction in her job as caregiver. Satisfaction for him as a recovering veteran.

"Cards will go late tonight. Won't be much time left for sewing."

"They only go late if you're winning. The odds are in my favor." She rolled up the magazine and gave him a swat on the arm.

He glanced down at the magazine.

"You're not blushing."

"I began with the letters to the editor. Part one of "The Regal Bachelor" can wait."

"Be sure to show me the picture." His voice held a hint of sarcasm. He pushed back on the wheels to turn around.

"I wasn't looking at pictures. There's a contest they're starting. A writing contest."

"Oh?" He repositioned his chair but didn't leave.

"The stories are two-part serials and the winner gets to have their story published in the *Companion* next March and April." She held out the page with the promotion. "There's a twenty-dollar prize with a free one-year subscription."

"Only twenty dollars?"

"The *Companion* goes all over the world. Besides, twenty dollars is a lot of money to some people."

"But not to me?"

"I didn't say that." She stood. A jolt of pain flooded her eyes. She grabbed the bedpost to steady herself.

"Sit down before you fall." Geoff maneuvered his chair closer to the bed.

"I won't fall." She was supposed to take care of him not the other way around.

"Then tell me about the contest. When's our story due?"

"Our? You mean my story." She gripped the wooden bedpost. "And I didn't say I was writing one. I'd be more than three weeks behind since Tubby was late with the mail."

He tapped his fingers on the arm of his wheelchair. "You didn't answer my question. When's it due?"

How could she flee from his inquisition with his wheelchair blocking her escape? His chair was like a dislodged boulder on a narrow logging lane.

"The editors have to receive the story by January first. If I did enter, I probably wouldn't win. I'm not a writer." She placed the magazine on the nightstand.

"Besides, my job is to take care of you."

He threw his hands in the air. "I'm taken care of, see?" He lowered his hands from his head to where his legs ended. "I'm the picture of health until you get to my stubby legs."

She held fast to her decision. "I'm not entering."

"Open that magazine." He pointed to the *Companion*. "Show me the illustration of the first story. That bachelor fellow."

She flipped to the first serial. The black and white picture showed a man and woman standing together in a garden.

"What's the man wearing?" he asked.

"A suit."

"Is he taller than the woman?"

"Yes."

"Handsome?" Geoff's eyebrows peaked.

She didn't answer.

Geoff waved his hand. "Flip to the next drawing."

She fanned the pages to where the next story began.

He strained his neck to get a glimpse of the people. "What's that man wearing?"

You just saw him. "A tuxedo."

"Is he taller than the—"

"Yes." She turned to the next illustration. What was his obsession with magazine models? "Aha! Here's a man in work pants and a simple cotton shirt, pining next to the bed of a sick woman. We don't know if he's tall." She showed Geoff the picture.

"That man's legs are huge. Never missed a meal. I'll bet he's strong, yet sympathetic."

"What does this have to do with my story?" She closed the magazine.

"I can't be those men."

"What do you mean? You could be just as handsome and well-dressed as these men." Her words cut off sharp. Did she believe Geoff was handsome? He was healthier since the morphine shots ended. And yes, he was the sort of man a girl could fancy. She shook her head to clear the thought from her mind.

"I can't pretend to be the men in those pictures. Without legs, I'm short and wheelchair bound." He leaned closer to her. "Write about me. Show the world an attractive stubby man."

Could she do that? "You're not stubby, and I'm not an author. Someone has to keep us fed. What if I fall behind on my chores?"

"We'll have pork and beans for dinner."

Counting the spider webs she needed to dust off the ceiling, she stalled. Why was this so important to Geoff? She tapped her foot. "All right, I'll try to submit a story." She looked over at his exuberant face. "I said try. And your legs aren't stubs."

He laughed. "Oh, yes they are. But at least I have someone shorter than me to keep me well-dressed."

She pressed a fist to her hip. "Then it's a deal."

"Cards? Now?" He backed his chair toward the door.

"Cards later." She steadied herself and headed toward the stairs. "First, I have to sew you some clothes for walking lessons." And she had to figure out what type of story she had just agreed to write.

~*~

Josephine stayed up past midnight constructing pants on the Singer sewing machine—a gift Mr.

Chambers had sent along to the lodge. She left Geoff downstairs on the couch with a stack of Kat Wil financial ledgers spread out around him. They had agreed to wait until morning for walking practice.

Before she retired for the night, Josephine sneaked downstairs to check on Geoff. He was in bed, asleep, his clothes crumpled in a pile beside the nightstand. His ledgers remained on the couch and coffee table. She dared not move them.

Someone else required her attention. The beast. Geoff wasn't around to object to her kindness. She plated leftover stew and set it outside the back door as a thank you to the dog for keeping her warm and comforted after the morphine incident. Climbing the stairs to her room, she put thoughts of that frigid night to rest.

In the morning, she swept her almost-shoulder-length hair into a bun. If Geoff was going to grip her collar, she didn't want anything in his way. Walking on wooden legs was the best medicine for Geoff. She trusted her gut. It's what they had wanted at the hospital.

Her palms started to sweat. What if he fell? Or worse, broke something? She would have to explain herself to Mr. Chambers. Heading downstairs, she tried not to think about Geoff crashing to the floor with strapped-on legs.

When she entered his room, he gave her a disgruntled grin. His right leg was already attached.

"I haven't seen you with your hair up." He buckled a strap on his chest.

She laid his new pants on the bed. "I didn't have much hair when we came to the lodge. It was cut off after—" She blocked the memory of Ivan's assault.

"With it up, you'll have a better grasp of my shoulder."

"You're going to walk in front? What are you, a glutton for punishment? Blue jaw not enough?"

"I don't want you falling and hurting yourself. What if you hit your head?"

"Then I lose the last year and a half of my life. The doctor gave me a two-year life sentence." He tapped his wrist. "Time's a wasting."

"Shut up." The words flew out of her mouth. How could he be so carefree about death?

He looked at her, eyebrows arched, eyes open wide.

Her cheeks flamed. "You don't know how long you have to live."

"Doc Miller said two years."

"That was before, when you were," she paused, searching for the right word, "sick." Picking up a bottle of oil from the nightstand, she sat beside him on the bed, and started rubbing a small amount onto the end of his left stump. "Only God knows how long we have."

"Is that your mother's wisdom?" He crossed his arms against his half-strapped chest.

"It's mine." She bent down and reached for his left leg. His stare gave the side of her face a sunburn. She swallowed hard. "God has numbered the hairs on our head, and He's numbered our days. Doc Miller isn't God."

"That's for sure." Geoff spit out his agreement as if he and the doctor didn't always see eye to eye.

Her own questions fluttered in her mind. Her first and foremost was why Doc Miller had prescribed endless morphine.

She slipped on his left leg, secured the straps, and

handed him his new pants.

"I'll work on a shirt and vest tonight. But please, no more talk about death." Images of Ivan's snarled face sent a chill across her skin.

Geoff bunched up the pant legs and fitted them over the shiny black shoes that bore no feet. "Don't fret, Jo. After June you won't have to worry about my peg legs."

How could he say such a thing? "I bet I will."

"No betting. Remember?" He grinned as he buttoned his pants at the waist and slowly stood.

I would bet on you. Every time. Her belly flip-flopped as she admired Geoff in his new clothes.

She focused on the task at hand and helped Geoff take a few steps toward the mirror.

"Can you tell?" Interest piqued in his voice. "About my legs." His chest and shoulders blossomed as his hands cinched his waist.

"Only by the way you walk, and that should improve with practice. Ready for a longer stretch?" She turned and felt his hands grip her shoulders. "Here we go—left, right, left."

"I'm done marching. Take it slow, and I'll try to keep up. If you feel a sharp pinch, you're going too fast." He brought his fingers together and squeezed her neck.

"Ouch." She rubbed her skin, having half a mind to race forward. Visions of split foreheads and broken arms cautioned her to behave.

"Grow an inch or two, would you? Then my arms could rest perfectly on your shoulders."

"You could shrink."

"I do that when my legs come off."

She stifled a chuckle. At least he displayed a sense

of humor.

He whistled as he fell in step behind her. "I'll try not to flatten the back of your boots."

"Good, because I didn't order a new pair from Tubby."

They shuffled into the living room, into the kitchen, and back into the living room.

As they passed her reading chair, he drew his index finger along the groove in the back of her neck.

She shivered. "Don't do that."

"Walking lessons are fun. Glad you suggested them." He sounded devilishly young and mischievous.

After a few laps through the lodge, she insisted he stroll around the furniture while she collected eggs. She watched from the kitchen as he lapped the sitting area. His concentration rivaled a toddler learning to walk for the first time.

When the hen coop was picked clean, she checked in on Geoff.

He lowered himself methodically onto the couch, at an angle, with measured breaths, letting his thigh support his weight.

"Not bad for starters." She strolled toward the couch.

"Help me take my legs off." He grimaced as he shifted to the edge of the sofa. "I don't want to rip my new pants. They're comfortable unlike that silly all-in-one."

Pride added an inch to her height as she headed toward the couch. He liked her flared pants. But then, any garment was better than his snap-crotch underwear.

She shimmied the material over his bolted-on knee and folded his pants, seams together.

When the straps fell and she began to remove the wood from his flesh, he stiffened.

Crimson circles ringed his stumps. The wood had gnawed on his skin, rubbing sections raw.

"You must have been in pain?" Oh, why did she push him?

"Pain is my companion." He gave her a lopsided smile.

"That's not funny."

She ran upstairs to get Dr. Miller's ointment. Geoff's pain was her fault. Why was there always a setback?

Settling down next to him on the couch, she massaged his leg and kneaded the menthol cream into the rash. The scent of sweet eucalyptus filled the room.

"Feels nice." His voice sounded as if he was drifting into a dream.

"We'll skip tomorrow. I don't want you to be in pain."

"This is normal. Except in the hospital when they forced us to walk, I didn't get personalized care. The nurses used to line us up in front of two rails. They'd cheer us on as if it was a competition to see who could waddle the gauntlet the fastest."

"Did you win?"

"I didn't try to. I didn't try at all."

He reached out and stroked the side of her neck. "You didn't flinch?"

"I must be getting used to being your balance beam." What did she care if he brushed a finger on her skin? She had to make sure his sore didn't get infected.

Geoff shifted his weight. "You can stop when you want."

"Not until I work this ointment into each tender

spot." What did she think she was doing pushing him to walk? She knew nothing about fake legs. Curse her stubbornness.

He sunk into the cushions. A moan rumbled from his lips. A sort of good moan. "Few more practices and I'll be able to inspect every tunnel at Kat Wil Mine."

Was he serious? She glanced at his face.

Eyes closed, his breaths deep and calm, he rested on the cushions as if he had just received a shot of morphine. Thank goodness, he hadn't.

Did he plan on traveling to Kat Wil Mine? The mine had been in his mother's family for years. It reminded him of his heritage. Kat Wil reminded her of something, too—her stepfather's murder. At that vile place, her stepfather gambled away all his pay and left her mother impoverished, working arthritic fingers to nubs. She'd find an excuse to avoid going to the mine. She'd stay at the lodge with the beast. And she'd explain it to Geoff one step at a time.

15

November came. Walking lessons continued and so did card games. She added an appendix to Dr. Miller's medical notebook documenting treatments for stump sores and morphine management. Geoff stayed mum on visiting Kat Wil Mine.

"I'd like to hear what you have written on your story." Geoff studied the cards in his hand. He stopped organizing his suits long enough to take a sip of his evening tea.

"No criticisms?" She collapsed the fan of her cards.

"How about a few critiques?" He folded his hand and leaned back on the couch like he was bloated from a starchy meal.

She laid her cards on the table. The sweat from her palm gave her pair of sixes a slight bend. What would it hurt to discuss her story? Geoff was educated and well read. She retrieved her notepad from her bedroom.

"The story is rough." Her words came out winded from the stairs. She sat back down without straightening her skirt. "My characters, Leonard and Ann—"

"Who?" He laughed. "This is a romance, right?"

"You don't like the names?" Her voice rose,

challenging his reaction. "Ann is my sister's name. She dated a clerk named Leonard."

"They're nice names, but plain and boring."

She blew out a breath. "What do you suggest?"

"How about a foreign name for the woman. Something French like Michelle, or Russian, say, um, Daria. Exotic names."

Her lips became a thin seam. How dare he insult her sister's name? And who was Daria? Was he remembering a nurse from the war?

"The woman can be tall with long blonde hair and a hint of an accent." He continued to comment on the woman's outfit.

Jo's fingernails almost ripped through her paper. "The lady is brunette. I will not write about a woman with yellow hair. Besides, the illustration will be in black and white. Dark hair shows better." Her head bounced for emphasis. "What men's names do you find exotic?" She emphasized his adjective.

"How about Gregory? Greg for short. A strong name." He repeated the name in various tones and accents.

She stood. "Why don't you read what I have written while I get us some more tea? I'm sure you'll have more criticisms."

"Critiques," he called as she left the room.

After filling his cup to the brim, she lounged in her chair and waited for more input.

"Greg has no legs?" He sipped his tea.

"Nope, not a one."

"Sounds familiar." He glanced her direction. "And Michelle..."

"Daria," she corrected.

"Yes, Daria…is the caregiver?"

"Uh huh."

"And how do they fall in love?" He scanned through the pages in his lap.

"They don't at first. Then he risks his life saving her from a grizzly bear." She waited for a hint of a reaction. Did he like it? Or was he still thinking of Christine or Michelle or some other girl. She relaxed her balled fists.

"And how does he rescue her from the bear without becoming dessert?"

She leaned in as if to share a secret, her elbows balancing on her knees. "He throws his wheelchair at the bear." She grinned. "With his muscular arms."

Geoff's mouth pulled to one side. "How does she respond?"

"I have to fill several pages, so she can't tell him of her feelings right away. I'm thinking maybe an eagle drops a love note or she ties the note to her wolf dog." Her eyes challenged him to comment.

"I imagine they get married, eat cake every day, end of story?" He shuffled the papers, shoved them her direction, and picked up his cards.

Had she offended him? All the stories in the *Companion* had a tidy ending.

"Yes." She thumbed the flimsy corners of the papers. "Greg and Daria have a nice life together."

"Then, you're writing a fairy tale, not a story." He studied his cards as if he hadn't seen them before. "Don't you think there are questions that need to be asked and answered? Answered honestly?"

Don't look at me like that. Not with those enlightened eyes.

"What do you mean?" Her pulse raced. Her eyes darted around the room, avoiding his inquisitive stare.

"Isn't there something she should ask him? Something she'd need to know if they married." His tone demanded an answer.

She thought about the conversations she had with Geoff. Was he referring to the two years Dr. Miller had prophesied? Silence filled the room. Her brain was fully empty.

Geoff drained his teacup. "Can he consummate the marriage?" He hesitated. "Father children?"

Her face burned hotter than scarlet embers. "I, uh…" The boom in her temples nearly burst through her brow. "I don't know," she stammered. *I don't want to know.*

"What if her heart's set on three kids, and he can't give her one. Will she give up motherhood to be with him? I've seen them, Jo. Men worse off than me. Cut nearly in half. Should we forget about them? Their hardship?" The roar of his voice was as ferocious as the bear's head above the mantel.

Her heart sank in her chest. "I'm sorry." Tears choked her voice. "It's…it's a made-up story."

Was he mad at her? The war? His injury?

She met his gaze.

"I can, you know." His words were whisper soft. "Have children."

Embarrassment prickled her skin. She would have sworn she had spiked a fever. "I can't talk about this." *I don't know how to talk about this.* "Greg and Daria won't either." She plunked her cup on the table and hurried toward the stairs. When she reached the landing, she turned to face him. "It's supposed to be a simple serial."

"You're writing a fairy tale, Jo, not a real story. Life's not a fairy tale." His voice held an addict's edge.

An edge that curled her toes into eagle's talons. The smashing of his teacup emphasized his words.

Papers in hand, she vaulted up the stairs at full stride. Almost at the top, her foot slipped. Her ankle twisted. The wooden stairs offered no cushion for her fall.

"Ahh." Air swooshed from her lungs. Pain ricocheted from her wrists to her knees. Rolling on her side, she investigated the sting in her throbbing ankle. Blood oozed through her stocking.

"Are you hurt?" Angst filled Geoff's voice. She heard him scrambling for his chair.

She braced herself against the railing. "I'm fine." But she wasn't. Her story was strewn on several steps. A drum beat of ache boomed up her leg. Her chest cinched from Geoff's inquisition.

Geoff wheeled into sight. "Let me—"

"Leave me be," she shouted as she limped up the last stair. "I'm done with your critique."

"Darn it, Jo." He slapped the wall. "I was being honest."

Closing her bedroom door, she sat on the bed and inspected her wound. Geoff could be honest with someone else.

She took gauze from the medical kit and held it to her cut. The bleeding stopped. With a one-footed hobble, she dressed for bed. Pulling the blankets up tight to her chin, she closed her eyes and concentrated on the black nothingness. She would not allow Geoff to upset her anymore today. If he called tonight, she would not answer. How dare he bring *that* up? She didn't want to know about *that*. Should she know about *that*? She did wonder about *that*.

When she opened her eyes, the alarm clock read

9:00 AM.

Her heart rallied as she rushed out of bed. Ouch! She lifted her ankle and pressed her lips together. Her sprain throbbed. She dressed in a hurry and hobbled downstairs as fast as she could without incurring another injury. Geoff read a ledger on the couch.

"Good morning," he said, closing his book. "There are some pancakes on the table for you. They might still be warm. It seems to be a late morning for both of us."

"Pancakes for me?" Was this an apology? She didn't see any shards of his shattered tea cup. "How did you manage to make them?"

"Ah." He sat straighter. "I tied a pipe I found under the sink to the spatula. I've been around a few flap jacks in my day." He eased into his chair.

Hiding the ache in her ankle, she sidestepped toward the table, sat, and placed a napkin in her lap. She tried a few bites.

"These are good." She poured more maple syrup onto her plate.

"Would you like some juice?" He wheeled closer.

"I'll get it." She beat him into the kitchen. After all, she was supposed to cook breakfast for him.

When she returned to the table, Geoff shifted a chair away, and perched alongside her. "I want to apologize for last night." His voice sounded like he was choking on a pancake.

Her attention stayed on her plate of food.

"I shouldn't have said the things I did." He tapped a nervous rhythm on his armrest. "Sometimes, I forget how old you are."

Enough already. "Apology accepted." She popped more breakfast into her mouth.

"You've gotten off to a good start on your story."

"I'm not going to finish the story," she said, while she sopped up syrup with a piece of pancake.

"Why not? What's more exciting than a leg-less Leonard?" He crossed his arms over his chest as if he was ready for more banter. She wasn't.

"I'm not naming him Leonard."

"Then you're learning already." He leaned toward her, a wily grin on his face.

Playing with the napkin in her lap, she tried to think of how she would explain her reasoning for quitting the contest. Her face warmed as he stared at her. "I don't know enough about certain things." He fidgeted as if he expected her to say more, but that was all she could muster on the subject of *that*.

"You have an older sister." He scratched his whiskers as if recalling Ann. "You must know something?"

His eyes felt like two lighthouse beacons aimed at her face. She gathered her silverware. "My mother says it is not appropriate for a lady to know until she is ready to marry."

"Oh, she does?" He rubbed his hand across his mouth, camouflaging his expression. "That doesn't mean you can't still write the story. You've seen and touched more places on a man's body than most married women. Unfortunately for you, it's been my cut off body and not those gents in the magazine."

She pounded the butt of her fork on the table. "I don't like it when you talk about yourself that way. There's nothing wrong with you."

His eyebrows arched. "I'm missing half my legs."

"I never knew you with legs. It's all the same to me." Same old injuries. Same old Geoff.

"Enter the contest." If he edged any farther off his chair he would fall in her lap. "Be honest about Greg's struggles. I'll only give my opinion if you ask for it, and I'll try to remember you're just an eighteen-year-old runt." A tease twinkled in his eyes.

"Fine." She tapped her healthy foot. "I'll try. And I'll try to remember what you've been through. Plus, those other veterans."

He laid his hand on hers. Warmth flooded her skin.

"I'll try to remember what you've been through, too," he said.

Was he talking about the lodge? His crinkled-brow expression concerned her.

"I don't understand."

"The men who tried to kill me were soldiers. German soldiers. My dad wasn't behind enemy lines pushing me into barbed wire."

She pulled her hand from his. "My stepfather didn't try to kill me. It was an accident. I fell."

"If you say so."

"It's the truth. I don't know what you've heard, but I was there." She didn't want to talk about the encounter with her stepfather. Geoff's closeness suddenly made her uneasy as though he was Marshal Dorsey's deputy.

She gathered her dishes and headed to the kitchen to clean them. She was not dredging up the scene in the Chamberses' bedroom.

Afterward, Geoff insisted on inspecting her ankle. She sat on his couch and propped her leg on the coffee table. Her scrape hardly compared with his bedsores, but he wheeled off to his room to find ointment and a bandage. He tied the cloth ends without looking as if she were a wounded trench mate.

"I want to believe you," Geoff said as he clipped the knot tails. "It's just that I feel responsible for this ankle, and I blame your stepfather for what happened to you that day."

Not this again. "Well then, you'll need to thank him, too. Because of him, I found my way to your mansion. Now, I'm here taking care of you."

He rocked the wheels of his chair back and forth.

"I am thankful." He smiled like he had beaten her at cards.

At his praise, her body sprouted wings and flew to the ceiling.

"I'm thankful my bedsores, bumps, and bruises are almost healed." He grinned, but she knew part of him was being serious.

"Don't say that. You'll jinx us." She wiggled her bandaged ankle. "And you haven't walked on your wooden stilts yet today."

~*~

On November 11, 1918, Tubby returned en route from Skagway to Juneau. He handed her a newspaper. Not letters. Not a magazine. Not a Butterick pattern. A newspaper. She read the headline three times. Each time she added a grateful "Amen." The Great War had ended. Germany had signed the armistice.

She rushed to show the paper to Geoff.

He read the headline in silence. "I'm glad it's over." His words were but a wisp. "I wish it would have ended sooner."

Her spirit grieved as she beheld his broken body. "Me, too, Geoff. Me, too."

16

"Gin," she called out, laying down a six and a ten of clubs on his run. They'd been playing cards for three days straight since Tubby brought news of the armistice. She welcomed talk of cards and points and not of fathering children or traveling to mines.

"How do you do that? You must cheat." Geoff tossed his cards on the coffee table.

"I do not. If you say that again, there'll be no more rummy." *What a blessing that would be.* She gathered the cards. "It's getting late, and I have dishes to finish."

"Is that suit coat almost done? Tubby said we had a week." Geoff re-positioned himself on the couch. He picked up a ledger from a pile on the floor.

The salmon from dinner had come back to life and was spawning in her stomach.

"What do you mean? Tubby said he wouldn't be back until spring."

Geoff concentrated on rows of numbers and dollar signs. "He said we could make a trip to the mine. Fall's been warmer than usual."

She dusted some lint from her chair. "The jacket's almost finished. Only a few buttons to go. If Tubby gives me enough warning, I'll even pack a lunch for the two of you."

"Three of us." He glanced up from the page. "I can't go to the lodge without you."

Her breaths shallowed. Had her lungs shrunk?

"You don't need me to go." Go to a place with gamblers, swindlers, and murderers? "You own that place. What do I know about mining?"

"You're going."

She shook her head.

He set his ledger on the couch, crinkled his nose, and stared at her as if she had insulted his card playing. "Why not? Are you afraid to be seen in public with me?"

If only that were the reason. She should admit to the lie but the hurt in his eyes made her heart sad.

"I never have been, nor ever will be, ashamed to be seen with you. I just can't go to Kat Wil. Not with you, not with anyone." She started to rise.

"Then I'm ordering you to accompany me. I pay you to meet my needs, and I can't balance on those wooden legs by myself."

"No." She snatched saucers from the table without looking at his face. "The dishes need washing."

He reached for her dress. "Get back here."

It was no use. He would follow her to the kitchen and argue until she gave in to his wishes. Grabbing her coat from a peg by the back door, she called, "I've got to check the hens." At least it would stall his barrage of reasons. Why couldn't he understand about the mine? It supplied her stepfather with alcohol, stole his good sense, his money, his life.

A light drizzle dampened her bangs as she ran to the hen house. The pulse of the bruise on her ankle reminded her how unpredictable Geoff Chambers could be. The *bluck-bluck-bluck* of disturbed hens greeted her as she slipped into the coop.

Minutes passed.

The squeak of the lodge door sent her heart into spasms. She recognized the cadence of Geoff's wooden limbs on the porch. He wouldn't try and maneuver the porch steps. Would he?

"What in the…?" Geoff's voice blended with the ring of a spinning dinner plate.

How could she have forgotten to bring in the beast's plate? Cards. That's how.

Peeking out from the hen house, she saw him clinging to the porch post for balance.

She rushed to help him.

He held up a hand to stop her.

Breathless, she waited on the bottom stair.

"Were you going to hide in the coop all night?" he asked. "It's getting dark."

"I might." Especially if he didn't let up about this trip to Kat Wil.

He lifted one of his wooden limbs and placed it on the next step.

Her stomach became a ball of yarn. She moved one stair closer.

"I can do this." He shifted the peg leg left on the porch. "You said I didn't need you."

Where she gripped the railing, her palm dampened. She had encouraged him to go alone, but seeing him totter on these steps caused her hair to go gray. "I did say that, but—"

He swept his back leg to the next step and stood statue still.

Jaw clenched, she rushed to his side.

"See, I'm learning." He flashed a prize-winning smile. "Though, I still need you to go to the mine with me. I can't...I don't want to go there without you." His eyes glistened.

Her spirit crushed.

"What if I fall, Jo? What if one of my legs gets twisted? Who's going to want to touch me?" He placed a hand on her shoulder as if they were beginning front facing walking lessons. His voice was so calm, so innocent. He could have negotiated the peace treaty singlehandedly. "People don't see me the way you do. They don't know what I need."

She tilted her head back and admired the stacked branches of a towering spruce. Mist feathered her cheeks. "I don't know if I can go to the mine."

"Come inside and talk to me. I'd like to avoid damp clothes...please."

She heard it. Was this the first time? She couldn't remember him using the "p" word before. Why did he have to use manners now when the thought of being around rough men, one of whom may have killed her stepfather, terrified her?

"No one is going to hurt you at the mine. Everyone at Kat Wil answers to me." He swayed on the step as if he anticipated a walk.

She steadied him. "My stepfather was murdered, possibly by one of your workers. What if he finds out I'm here on the island? Alone. With you. What if he thinks I have money?"

"This is my house." Geoff stabbed the post with his index finger. "Anyone trespassing has to come through me."

"I know." Her tone added a "but." She tried not to think about the disadvantages of his condition.

"Guns even the field. I'm a crack shot. I've had plenty of shooting practice. If someone so much as flinches in these woods, he'll die." He leaned outward as if addressing the trees. "Hear that world? This is a shootin' lodge."

"Stop yelling. You'll wake Mr. Gilbertsen's ghost."

He put an arm around her shoulders. "We're going to Kat Wil—owner and assistant."

"Assistant?" The title sounded important. "Can I still think about it?" He enfolded her into his fleece jacket. Her protest was cut off by a warm chest pressing against her face. The hearty scent of cinnamon and all-spice filled her senses. "Did you eat more ginger snaps?"

"I left you one." Geoff began to chuckle then went rigid. Through her coat sleeve, his fingers pinched her skin. "I need the rifle," he whispered.

Was there a stranger at the lodge? Turning, she saw the threat. Not a man. But the beast. Her beast, jogging merrily toward the porch.

17

"Get inside." Geoff pushed her toward the door. "I'm going to take care of that animal once and for all."

"Don't you dare." She dropped her weight, making it harder for Geoff to push her up the steps. "He hasn't hurt anyone."

"Not yet. Now move." Anger sizzled in his voice.

She rounded on him. "I will not allow you to shoot that dog. He kept me warm when you locked me out of the lodge. If it wasn't for his fur, I'd have been a block of freezer ice."

"You let that thing near you?" He glanced at the plate on the porch. "You've been feeding it too, haven't you? That's why I have china outside my back door."

A moaning howl interrupted their discussion. The beast sat on the path, his snout skyward. He gurgled a low rambling bark. He seemed to be telling his side of the story.

Stepping away from Geoff, she jogged down the stairs and toward the beast.

"Get back here." Geoff's command reached the tallest evergreens.

The beast rubbed against her coat, using her leg as a de-furring post. She stroked its long, damp back. "Someone abandoned this dog. He's not mean." She looked at Geoff who had shifted to the top stair. "I feel better having him around after what I told you about my stepfather. He's protection."

"I can protect you, Jo." The tone of his voice almost had her convinced. "And I have a right to know what's going on in my house." He pointed at the beast. "But I don't—"

"I'll go to the mine." Her words came out so fast the beast sprang to attention. She'd do anything to keep Geoff from harming her newfound friend. "Promise me you won't shoot him."

Geoff stepped toward the door. He shifted one leg then the other.

Was he getting the rifle even after her plea?

"No more secrets," he spoke as if he issued an order and then jabbed a finger at the plate. "No more booby traps."

She nodded while rubbing the beast's ears. She didn't want to go to the mine, but if it kept her dog alive, she'd let Geoff win. Just this once.

~*~

The *Maiden* arrived on November 20, 1918, to make the trip to Kat Wil Mine. Thank goodness for her birthday bolt of material. She had finished a voile frock with a loose belt and V-neck that would be suitable for the visit. When she opened the door, Tubby lumbered inside with a Royal typewriter in one arm and a pair of black leather boots in the other.

Tubby handed her the shoes. "I've got to be north of Yakutat before the storms. We best get a move on, you two."

"Storms?" She peeked out the front door at the

horizon.

"Not 'til tonight." Tubby set the typewriter on the coffee table. He turned to address Geoff. "Found a walking stick for you in Ketchikan. It'll help you navigate the mine."

"I've got Jo for that, but thanks all the same."

"We'll take it," she said. "Who knows if we'll need a weapon?"

The men laughed. She didn't. Her jest could become a reality.

She admired the gold buckles on the gifted boots. "How did you know I needed shoes? These heels will keep my hem out of the mud."

Tubby puffed on his pipe. "I have a wife at home. She can't fit those no more. Figured you could."

Josephine sat in her chair and changed her shoes.

"The men won't be looking at your feet, so stay close." Geoff's stern features cautioned her as if he were a teacher and she a tardy student. "We leave by 2:00 PM, Captain's orders."

"Sure you don't want to bring the chair?" *Please change your mind.*

Geoff shook his head. "I've got you."

Rising, she positioned herself in front of him, took his hand and placed it on her shoulder. "Then balance away."

Tubby had nailed planks on the gangway so Geoff could board the ship. His descent required two burly men to keep him from plunging face first into the deck. He sprawled on a bench in the steering room, log-legs straight out in front of him as he pored over surveys of the mine.

She focused on the mountain peaks frosted white with heaven's snow and watched for the movement of wildlife among the timbers of the island. The trip was short. No time to fret over the possibility of storms thrashing the *Maiden* and swallowing up the boat and crew.

For her, Kat Wil Mine had been a place of mystery. A place across the channel where her stepfather worked and lost his pay. Ivan refused to take the girls anywhere near it. "No place for a lady" he used to say. How would he feel if he knew she was going there with the owner?

The *Maiden* slowed near the clear-cut slope of a mountain. Buildings spotted the various levels of the mountainside, lining the shore for what seemed like miles. Water plunged from long horizontal sluices, soaking piles of tailings waiting below. Crushed rock piles stood taller than some of the buildings but not the massive buildings nearest the dock. Those buildings had rows of windows, eyes to see who came on strange ships.

On deck, she took a deep breath, inhaling the scent of dank, cut pine. Her lungs froze when she noticed the wooden stairs leading from one level of the mine to the next. How could Geoff tour the mine? Office work must be on the schedule.

"Morning's passing us by." Geoff rose with Tubby's help and placed a hand on her shoulder. The other hand held the walking stick like a baton.

The crew supervised Geoff's disembarking until he was clear of the ship. Marty Hill waited at the end of the dock with another man—both dressed in double-breasted coats.

As she and Geoff approached their greeting party, Marty closed the gap and took her hand. "It's a pleasure to see you again Miss. Nimetz. May I introduce my assistant, Mr. Collins?"

"How do you do?" She swallowed a smug smile. Geoff had an assistant now, too.

Geoff leaned forward for handshakes. His grip tightened on her shoulder.

Marty led them inside the main building—a windowless box that felt more like a cave than a manager's office. All the furnishings were wooden—desks, side bar, and four chairs. The electric light did its best to enliven the dreariness of the stark wood, but the room still had a coffin-like aura. She stationed herself in a corner, out of the way of the desks, but near enough to assist Geoff if he needed to stand.

Geoff, Marty and Mr. Collins perused ledgers and maps and discussed neighboring mines.

"Absolutely no cave-ins." Geoff's fist pounded the desk. "Or strikes."

"We'll try our best," Marty assured him.

"You'll do your best." Geoff's demanding voice had made her cry at the mansion. Funny how the men jumped and she didn't. "I know of superintendents that would snatch your jobs like a stray ten-dollar bill." Geoff sat military straight in his chair.

Marty nodded. "I believe we know the same people." He inspected the map as if seeing it for the first time.

When Geoff's remarks couldn't be heard all the way back in Juneau, Marty slid open the door to the side bar and withdrew a bottle of whiskey.

"It's almost noon. Not too early to whet our whistles, is it gentlemen?" Marty raised a glass. "Miss. Nimetz?"

Alcohol? During work? She shivered, and not from the draft. Visions flashed in her mind. Drunken holiday fights. Smashed dinnerware. Hiding upstairs in Ann's arms.

Displeasure wrinkled Geoff's forehead. "Jo...sephine and I will have tonic water."

After two shots of whiskey, Marty locked the cabinet. "We'd better get started with the inspections. It's been awhile since you've been here, Mr. Chambers, and you're leaving early afternoon."

"Because of the storms." She whipped on her coat and dutifully positioned herself near Geoff while Marty donned a jacket. Geoff's hand rested on her shoulder pads.

They shuffled toward the door as practiced. Walking stick, step, hold steady. At the threshold, the stick caught. Geoff stumbled. She stiffened. Her heart rate spiked and made her glands sweat like it was August.

Geoff's hand dropped to her hip for balance, and stayed. Stayed for a healthy minute.

Thank goodness for a thick coat lining.

Marty studied Geoff's hand placement. Studied her reaction. And studied everything in between. Her muscles tensed with the swipe of his gaze.

"Marty, you're going to have to level this threshold." Geoff's hand returned to its normal spot on her shoulder. He urged her forward. "We best keep moving."

"We have to leave by two." She reminded everyone within ear shot.

At each site they visited, men appeared. They gawked at her and Geoff. She gawked back. Did any look familiar? She didn't recall a one. A layer of dirt camouflaged the miners' faces.

All the buildings seemed the same, plain, planked,

and brown. Nothing caught her attention except the torture of her new hand-me-down boots. With every step, the stiff leather scraped skin from her toes. No wonder Tubby's wife had given the heels away.

They headed toward the bunk houses. Thank goodness their last stop was near the dock. A screen door shared the dormitory's stench of musty body odor with the outside world. Marty meandered down the central hallway. She followed and gripped each finger-printed door frame to mask her hobble.

In one of the rooms, a lone man laid in a top bunk. When Marty greeted the miner, he sprung up, and dangled his legs over the side of the bed. Geoff patted the mattress.

"How do you like your new bed?" Geoff tapped the frame with his new balancing stick.

The miner didn't acknowledge Geoff. His eyes were on her, inching up and down her torso as if he was calculating her dress size. Her stepfather was right. She shouldn't have come.

"Nice," the man said turning his attention to Geoff. "My bed. This one right here is wonderful."

The wink aimed her direction rattled her composure. She turned abruptly, dipped out of Geoff's hold, and stepped into the hallway. How dare that miner gaze at her like a holiday roast? A murmuring of male voices cut short her indignation. A group of dusty-faced, dusty-haired men approached. They must have been in the tunnels, for they looked as if they had been sprinkled with pollen.

The crowd swarmed her space. Lint from their clothing filled the air along with the stench of sour sweat. Josephine coughed. She had to get out. Get outside.

Returning to the bunk room, she clutched Geoff's arm. "Geo…Mr. Chambers, we need…we need to be on our way."

He kept talking.

Was she dreaming? No. This would be a nightmare. Sweat drenched her bangs. "I'm feeling faint." She heard her own declaration, but didn't know who she said it to since it seemed as if she was floating above the floor with bumblebees swarming on her skin.

Immediately, Geoff broke off his conversation. He wrapped an arm around her waist. Marty supported her from the other side.

"Clear the way," Marty yelled.

Men snapped to attention along the wall.

"Don't go down on me, Jo."

The *thunk* of Geoff's walking stick echoed in her head.

Outside the bunk house, she collapsed on a clear-cut stump. Wintery puffs of smoke emerged from her mouth. Fingers kneaded her shoulder. She glanced upward. Geoff stood guard above her.

"See," she said, "you should have left me at the lodge." She stilled his hand. "I won't topple you now that I'm outdoors in the fresh air."

"Are you sure?" His head dipped down to examine her eyes.

"I'm well—"

Thwack.

The door to the bunk house flew open. Men filed out.

"Mr. Chambers?" a bushy-lipped man shouted.

Where was Marty?

Geoff acknowledged every man with a nod before

he answered. "This isn't a good time. My assistant is ill."

"We heard talk of more pay at Trident," the mustached man continued to speak. "You here to raise our pay?" Agreement echoed his request.

"Half of Trident collapsed. They have to pay high wages to keep workers." Geoff paused and scanned the crowd again. "But if Trident raises their wages, I'm sure Mr. Hill will inform me, and we'll follow suit. Otherwise, September is when wages will be adjusted."

"It's a shame the Chambers family can't hire all our children to keep 'em fed." The insult came from the leering mattress man.

"Your boy ain't near as pretty as her," a heckler called out.

"How old are you, gal?" another miner asked.

"Old enough," someone shouted.

Strangers laughed. Laughed at her. Laughed at the signer of their paychecks.

Anger spiked through her veins. Her hands fisted, quaking with outrage. She didn't need charity. The Chambers family needed her services not the other way around.

She stood on the stump. Her raw toes burned as boot leather grazed her skin.

"Shut your mouths, all of you." The shriek in her voice sent an eagle darting from a nearby pine.

Stunned faces went slack-jawed.

"Shame on you for spreading lies. How can you jeer at an outstanding veteran like Mr. Chambers? After my stepfather's death, he paid my mother wages Ivan hadn't even earned yet. If Ivan had brought home his paycheck instead of gambling with you, my family would be better off." Her chest heaved. Stored up emotion rattled her rib cage. "I am a nurse. A good nurse. And an assistant to Mr. Chambers."

Bewildered eyes gawked at her.

A few men apologized.

"Don a nurse's cap for me. Will ya?" a voice in the crowd bellowed.

"Odds are against you," someone cackled.

Her cheeks flamed. "It's because of the likes of you Ivan was murdered."

The rumblings quieted.

"One of you shot him," she shouted.

Her hand flew to her mouth. She had spilled the truth.

Salt water flooded her tear ducts. No way was she going to break down and sob in front of these buffoons. The little girl inside of her was already hiding in a bed, in a closet, in an alley behind a saloon.

She hopped off the stump and fled.

Sprinting down the shore toward Marty's office, she turned a corner and leaned against the side of a building. Small talk with Mr. Collins would be a chore. She eased the weight off her throbbing feet, collapsed against the wood wall, and wished she could forget her outburst.

Starlight specks blurred her vision. She bent over to clear her head.

"Miss. Nimetz?"

Her hand shot to her heart.

"Didn't mean to give you a start, Miss." A man stood a few feet away. His gaze never met hers. Instead, it traveled back and forth, from the office building to the building next door.

"Have we met?" She didn't remember him from

the bunk house.

"I knew Ivan...your Pa." He stepped closer, his red-rimmed eyes intent on her face.

"Oh," was all she could say. A shiver stole the warmth from her body. She struggled to wet her mouth, but her tongue was rough and dry like days old rags.

"I wanted to say how sorry I was 'bout the whole thing." He came closer. Too close. His size dwarfed her. "It was a tragedy. Nothing I could do. Ivan placed one bet too many."

There was a drumming in her brain. Danger, danger, danger. But how could she run with a giant stationed before her and with her bum feet?

"Thank you for your condolences." Her words came out faint and breathy. Her gaze darted toward the office. "Someone's coming," she lied.

The man scratched his chin. "Do you remem—"

"Where have you been?" Geoff's words filled the alley.

She bumped her head against the wall.

Praise be! She should reprimand her boss for his surly disposition, but in this moment, his ranting was a symphony.

Geoff stabbed the ground with his walking stick as if he meant to slay the earth.

The nearer he strutted, the happier she became.

"What did you think you were doing running off like that? Marty Hill will never lead me around by the arm again. Do you hear me?" He seized her shoulder. "You abandoned me."

Geoff glanced at the awe-struck miner. "Who are you?"

"Young," he stammered. "Edgar Young."

"Well, Mr. Young, get to work."

The stunned miner backed away. His head bobbed in her direction.

"Thank you for your kind words," she said, but the man didn't answer.

"How could you run off like that?" Geoff's hand still grasped her shoulder, but he balanced on his new cane.

"I'm sorry. I got flustered. It won't happen again." She clasped her hands to keep them from shaking.

"Darn right, it won't. You're going to sit in that office until it's time to leave. Hear me?"

All of Kat Wil could hear him.

She nodded. "I'm ready to leave when you are." Ready as ever.

18

Later that afternoon, Tubby carried her into the lodge. "It's my fault for giving you those fancy buckle-ups. You'd be in better shape if you crawled around the mine. Next time wear your chicken coop boots."

"Yes, Father."

A smile lit up Tubby's whiskered face as he placed her on the couch. "I can't stay. Clouds are rolling this way."

"I'll take it from here." Geoff accompanied Tubby to the porch. When he returned, he leaned against the edge of the couch. "Assessed the damage yet?"

"Not yet. I'm afraid to look." She slid the leather over the tops of her feet and fought back tears. Dried blood and clumps of dead skin adorned her toes. The blisters on her heels stung for attention.

Geoff teetered toward the kitchen.

"Where are you going?"

He steadied himself with a chair. "You need to soak those feet."

"I'll get the water." She tried to stand.

"You most certainly will not. Get back on that couch. That's an order."

"You can't give me orders."

"Yes, I can. Even if you don't follow them."

Distant thunder caught her attention.

"Did you hear that?" she asked over the rush of the faucet.

"I told you this morning there'd be storms tonight." Geoff used the dining table to brace himself. He cradled a Dutch oven in the crook of his arm. After a few awkward steps, he handed her the container.

"I cook in that," she said.

"Extra flavor. Now soak."

She set the oven on the floor. Her feet hovered over the warm water before slowly sinking into the pot. Her skin sizzled until the pain became a comfortable ache.

Thunder sounded a few miles away. Looking for cover, she grabbed a decorative pillow and buried her face in the material. The cloth smelled like Geoff's bath soap—lye with lemons.

Geoff sat beside her, towel in hand.

She gave him a side-glance. "Is the dog out back?"

"That thing is on the porch—for now."

"Good." She relaxed into the dark brown cushions.

When her feet resembled large prunes, Geoff dried them. He gently patted her toes. If he pressed too hard, she did a backward push up.

A lightning flash lit up the bay window.

She covered her eyes with the pillow again. It didn't matter to her if Geoff thought she was silly, she didn't want to see the storm.

"Lean back." He lifted her feet from the floor and settled them on his lap.

As she rotated to rest lengthwise on his couch, she didn't complain about his bossiness. After all, he let her lounge in his special spot.

He massaged her sore arches without being bribed

with pancakes or ginger snaps.

Her less injured pinkie toe jiggled.

"You have the tiniest toes."

She peered over the pillow. "Not every part of me is tiny, small, runtish..."

"That's not a word," he said.

Thunder boomed over the lodge. She gasped and reunited her face with the pillow. She concentrated on the trails Geoff was tracing on her feet. His closeness calmed her fears. Somehow, in his company, she didn't envision the storm demolishing the lodge.

Geoff's fingers circled her ankles. "Why do storms bother you so much? You've lived in Alaska your whole life, haven't you?"

He massaged the length of her calves. The long, tingling pathways he made on her legs felt so good after a day of trudging all over the mine.

"I got caught in an electrical storm when I was a little girl." She shifted and repositioned her neck on the fat armrest.

"Why didn't you take cover?"

Her body stiffened. She wanted to erase that memory, not share it with Geoff. "I was waiting for someone."

"In the rain?" he asked, surprise in his voice.

"No." Did he think she was stupid? "In an alley where there was an overhang." *Stop interrogating me.* She clutched the pillow as if it could be a shield from his twenty questions.

The long strokes of his hands rose to her knees.

"Were you waiting for Ivan?"

Cool air pimpled her skin. Her heartbeat quickened. Was it because he'd brought up Ivan or because of the touch of his hands along her legs?

Her fists crushed the edging on the pillow. His ministration crested her knee caps. "I was waiting at the saloon. And there was an overhang." The words raced out of her mouth.

"You said that." His firm hands glided the length of her legs from her ankles to her knees, flirting with the hem of her dress.

She was positive someone was fanning themselves in her stomach, fanning themselves with chickadee feathers. She had to stop his massage, or she might fly away. Straight. Into. The. Ceiling.

Reaching out, she grabbed his hand as it circled her knee. Her job was to take care of his injuries. Nothing more. Not like those men at the mine insinuated. She met his faraway gaze.

"I won't go any higher." His fingers traveled down her legs retracing their path, tickling her skin. "I miss my legs." He didn't look at her. "I miss the mundane things; crossing my legs in a chair, curling my toes in a rug, river water splashing on my ankles."

The storm's fireworks brightened the inlet, but she did not cover her face.

"I used to chase my brother Bradley, catch him in my arms, lift him high in the air." He shook his head. "No more."

"I'm so sorry." She watched as he envied the legs draped over his uneven thighs. "I wish it hadn't happened. Not to you. Not to anyone."

Gently, he shifted out from under her. "Speaking of legs, it's about time mine come off."

"Let me help you?" She wedged her pillow into the corner of the couch.

He held out his hand to stop her. "I've got this. Give your feet a rest."

When he had gone, she cautiously placed her feet on the floor. The menthol ointment had doused the fire in her toes.

"Jo, I hate to bother you, but I need your help. I shanked the strap in the buckle. I'd use the mirror to fix it but my left leg's already off."

Hobbling to his room, she chuckled about their leg predicaments.

She grabbed the bunched strap and wiggled the material. "You wedged it good this time." Gritting her teeth, she pulled, hard. The cloth came loose. "There it is."

Geoff lounged on his bed. "I'd call you a saint, but you shouted down your elders today."

Tension tightened her chest. "Don't even start about the mine."

"Why not? I liked the 'outstanding veteran' part." His straight face creased into a grin.

"Glad someone liked it." She turned to leave.

"Jo," his voice became serious, "about that man at the mine."

Her posture stiffened. "You mean Mr. Young?"

"I checked the roster. There isn't an Edgar Young working at Kat Wil." His eyebrows arched high on his forehead. "The man probably works there. I can find out who he is and get his name."

She thought for a moment. "We have no proof to accuse him of being involved in a murder." She chewed her lip. "My family's name would be in the paper again. Mother would fret if they mentioned the gambling." She shook her head. "It won't bring Ivan back. With all your ranting, I doubt he'll come near this place." She turned and walked delicately toward the bedroom door. "Tea before Gin Rummy?"

"What happened to your real father?" Geoff's tone was humble, almost a whisper.

The question stopped her short. She couldn't remember the last time she had spoken about her father. "He died in a lumbering accident when I was two years old. Joseph…Joseph Jensen was his name. I don't recall much about him. My mother brings out a drawing of him on our birthdays."

"I think he'd be proud of your trip today." Geoff laid his right leg on the floor. "If you'd like, after I beat you at cards, you can sleep on the couch in my room tonight. In case you're worried about visitors or the storm."

She stood a hair taller. "Thank you, but I'm feeling rather safe." Remembering his rant at Mr. Young put a smile on her face. "And rather blessed." *And not only at cards.*

19

"Didn't know I was an excellent typist, did ya?" Geoff tapped his fingers on the keys, chanting "ASDF." The chant soon turned to "Greg and Daria."

"I didn't know that a trip to Kat Wil would give me time to write." She wiggled her toes, grateful that they were almost healed.

"You write too fast. I can't find a single comma." He squinted at her handwritten page as if it needed deciphering.

"My grammar's not that bad." She looked down at her journal and noticed she had written the same phrase twice.

"It's not that good."

"Math's my strong suit and—"

"Not rummy?" He chuckled.

She clenched her teeth and pointed her pencil at him as if he was her student. "Someone had to help my mother fill orders. You didn't have to worry about feeding a family." She had said too much. If Geoff hadn't gone off to war, maybe he would have gotten married, fathered a child. Her cheeks scalded. Resting her pencil in her lap, she continued to write.

"Here." Geoff handed her the pages. Was he

refusing to help her? "I don't have to provide for a family, but at least I know how to diagram a sentence. Why don't you read them to me?"

"I'm sorry if…"

"Just read." He held claw-like fingers above the keys.

She began to read slowly. Slow enough for him to keep up:

Her welcoming "Good Morning" did not ring through the lodge. "Daria," Gregory called, wheeling through the kitchen—his eyes searching out back. He stopped at the bottom of the stairs. "Daria?"

A faint voice uttered words he could not recognize. He waited, not wanting to burst into her bedroom sanctuary. Minutes passed. Riddled with concern for her well-being, he sat on the first step, and pushed his body up the stairs. He called her name one last time before opening the door. His heart pounded with fear as he glimpsed her frame. Her face flushed crimson with fever. Her brown eyes, sunken and dazed, stared at him as if they didn't recognize him.

"Gregory," she moaned, her lips dry and cracked. "Leave me be. I can't take care of you if you get the sickness."

"I'm feeling sick too," he interrupted. "My reading tastes do not include women's serials."

"You're reading this one."

"Out of necessity."

She huffed and continued:

His vigil lasted two days. Exhausted from little sleep, he slumped in a chair near her bed. She slept comfortably now. No outbursts of tears like when she burned with fever.

He must have dozed off for a while, for when he awoke, she beheld him with the hint of a smile. Her breathy voice, light as air, confessed, "I love you, Gregory."

If only her confession were true and not muddled from sickness.

"Hah! Does he get the flu too so he can blurt out his love while ill with fever?"

"No, he does not." She folded the pages and pretended to swat his arm.

"When does Greg propose?"

She wished he would do more typing and less talking. "Soon."

"Let me guess. On one knee with a big diamond ring?"

"Did you read ahead?" she asked.

"Nix the one knee. My legs don't work that way, and there would be no way on earth I'd propose without them. I'm going to look like one of those gents in the *Companion*."

She rubbed her forehead. "Fine. They'll go to the waterfall. He'll be in the chair he threw at the bear."

"Repaired, is it?"

"Stop changing the story. I have to get it finished and in the mail and to Ohio in a month's time." And take care of you. And the holidays are coming. And why did she want to do this? The dull throb of a headache traveled across her forehead. She slumped in her reading chair.

He held out his hand for the story pages. "You write. I'll type."

The words she had written didn't seem to make sense anymore. She crossed out the last sentence.

Geoff thumbed through the pages.

"Daria tells Greg she loves him and then turns down his proposal?"

Her head rocked back and forth against the headrest. "We talked about this before, remember? He can't have children. She wants children. No marriage, at least not now."

"Well, they could..."

"I'm not discussing this. You suggested he was..." She stammered trying to come up with the appropriate word. "Because of his injuries, he can't be a father." The warmth in her cheeks was now a blazing fire of embarrassment. The tips of her fingers even glowed scarlet.

Geoff's cheeks didn't turn red, but they did plump. His chest shook as he struggled to hide his amusement. "Now, I need a tissue. This is a heart breaker."

"We need to keep going."

"Then read to me again. Greg's got to get back on his feet." He sputtered a laugh.

She rubbed her forehead and read.

As she walked toward the shore, she turned and looked at the lodge one last time. It was then she saw him, half-hidden behind the bedroom sheers. Her heart sank deep in her chest as their gazes met. She never thought she would fall in love with him.

She stared at the ship, its rope ladder cascading down to the waves. A burly man rowed a small boat ashore, the shallow water too perilous for the mighty ship. He helped her load her suitcase, lifting her with ease over the side of the small row boat. Her stomach lurched with every rock of the craft. As they neared the ship, the crewman steadied the dinghy and handed her the ladder. Her body froze. She could not stand or will her feet to move.

"Take me back!" she cried.

"Just like a woman, can't make up her mind. Leaves poor Greg wounded and flailing in the dirt."

"Oh, please, now you're being dramatic. The war

imagery is a bit much." She put down the pages. "The story must be growing on you."

"I haven't read the ending." He sipped his tea.

"That's because I haven't written it."

"Then hurry up and get this poor guy a wife."

~*~

She finished the story on December fifth. Geoff had promised he would type it straightaway. Hopefully, a musher would stop by soon to post the mail. She wasn't taking any chances with a January first deadline. Filling out the entry form, she decided to title her story *Alaskan Desires*.

That night, the typewriter clicks slowed then stopped. Geoff picked up a page of her story and shook it in the direction of her chair. Still holding the paper, he began to read out loud:

Her cherry lips pressed into his as tears streamed down her powdered face. Her mouth moved in unison with his, enjoying their passion. Their union could not be broken as his love held her there to share the sweetness of their new life together.

"I can't fight my love for you, Gregory," she breathed, holding his face in her hands.

Geoff rubbed his jaw. "This is not you." His stare made her heart spasm.

"What do you mean?" Her back straightened, broadening her shoulders. "I wrote every word myself. And I did not copy anyone's story."

"It's too grown up. Did your sister tell you what to write?" His accusatory tone had her on her feet.

She unbuttoned the sleeve on her dress and wrenched back the material, displaying an arm dotted with broken blood vessels. "I've read a lot of serials, but I've never kissed a boy. This scene I practiced on my arm."

He buried his face in his hands. "What will your mother say? Or my father? Maybe this wasn't a good idea after all. I'm supposed to be looking out for you. You're my responsibility while you're here at the lodge."

"I am not your responsibility. You're my responsibility. I take care of you." Did he believe people would get the wrong idea about their relationship? Not everyone retrieved their thoughts from the gutter like the miners at Kat Wil. She wouldn't change her story. Not one word.

She sat in her chair and crossed her legs. "Eighteen-year-olds are beyond lullabies and children's fables."

"Well, you need to change the ending," It sounded like an order. "Daria's pregnant. Do you know how that happens?"

She played with her hair trying to shield her face from his penetrating blue eyes. "Yes." She hated the wobble in her voice. Thank goodness for Ann's letter. "Daria and Greg marry and fortunately for them, the doctors were wrong about Greg's condition."

He drummed his fingers on the table.

"If anyone questions the story, they can blame me. I encouraged you to write it." He held her gaze a little too long for her comfort—especially with the topic at hand. "I do have responsibilities where you're concerned. You live under my roof, and I've seen more of this crazy world than you have."

"Yes, you have." She didn't want him to stay so serious. "And I have an obligation to this world to show them a man who has more to offer than big shoulders, big arms, and a big wallet. Now, keep typing."

And to her amazement, he did.

20

An Aleut musher, covered in seal skin and wolf fur, arrived on December tenth, leaving plenty of time for her story to make it to the editorial office before New Year's Day. The musher left cards and packages on the porch, refusing to come in for tea. His narrow, scouting eyes scanned the lodge with suspicion. He signaled his dog team to move on the minute his boots hit his sled's footboards.

Geoff seemed amused at the young man's unease. "Guess there's talk even among the natives about this place. Next time the mail's delivered, I'm going to borrow that white afghan of yours and pretend to be Mr. Gilbertsen's ghost."

"You'll do no such thing." She bent down to pick up the packages. "If it wasn't for that musher running a team through the snow, we'd have no gifts for Christmas and there'd be no cards for your birthday."

"I'm not celebrating my birthday."

"Yes, you are. We need to celebrate. There's been very little sun and fun around here."

"What are you talking about? I enjoyed typing your serial. And we had plenty of laughs over that goose you cooked for Thanksgiving." He wheeled toward the dining table with a lap full of letters to sort.

"You just want a reason to eat cake."

"What's wrong with that? Besides your family will be expecting some kind of celebration for your birthday and Christmas." *And they will give me a reprieve. Maybe a holiday bonus when they see how well he's doing.*

"My family will be in San Francisco. I told my father to go with Julia and celebrate with her family. Bradley will have more fun in Frisco." He stopped sorting mail to open a card.

"Well, what about my family?" She set a box of his on the dining table.

"What about them? I told you I wasn't up for visitors."

"Then I'll go to Juneau for a short visit. I'll only be gone a day or two. I can leave food already prepared."

His head snapped her direction. "I'm not staying here alone."

She clutched a package her mother had sent. How she wished she could reciprocate in person. "You could come with me." She began envisioning the arrangements. Geoff could sleep on a cot. Borrowing one from a neighbor wouldn't be a problem.

"No." His tone was definite. He continued reading as if the discussion were over.

It wasn't.

She set her gift on the stairs, whisked into the dining room, and gripped the chair closest to Geoff. Pulse racing, bracing for a fight, she blurted out, "Why not? Is it because of where I live?"

He squinched his nose. "I've never seen where you live. Can't you leave me be?"

"But it's Christmas." Desperation whined in her voice.

"Fine, visit your family."

Her shoulders relaxed.

"But don't bother coming back. I need someone I can depend on."

She ripped the envelope from his hands. "How can you say that to me?" She hardly recognized her voice through the breathy squeaks. "After all I've done for you."

He jerked his chair back from the table. "I'm not staying at your mother's house." He continued before she could protest. "Or anyone's house for that matter. I'd like to keep my dignity."

"What's that supposed to mean?"

"I grunt. I grunt to get on the toilet. I grunt to get into bed. And what about my bath. How would your mother feel seeing you touch a half-naked man when he gets out of the tub? Tell me that, Jo."

"She wouldn't mind. You're covered."

"Barely. You rub ointment on my backside."

"Not as much. Lately." Her cheeks warmed.

"What if she won't let you come back to the lodge?" He gave her an ah-hah stare.

"She would." But she may not. Geoff wasn't Mr. Gilbertsen whose main need was comfort and fluids. "We could stay at your place?"

He swiped his hands over his face as if he was embarrassed by what he asked her to do. Shaking his head, he said a deadpan, "No."

Tears welled in her eyes. She had committed to staying at the lodge until June.

"I'm going to open my gift." She turned and took the stairs two at a time.

She shut the door to her bedroom. Hurry up, June. Hurry up, *Companion.* Hurry up, life. And what was her life going to be like after June? Had her customers gone elsewhere? Her breaths ached. She stood rooted to the throw rug, staring at the ceiling.

Shhh-kunk. Shhh-kunk. Shhh-kunk.

What was that? It sounded like the drag of a sack of flour.

He wouldn't.

Staccato wheezing grew louder.

Her muscles tensed as she opened the door.

Geoff lay on his side. His arms pulled his torso upward while his stumps cleared a stair. A wind gust breath escaped from his mouth.

"Are you insane?" She hurried down the staircase. She sat on the stair above him and blocked his ascent. "If you fell—"

"You'd get to go to Juneau for Christmas." He grabbed the railing and pulled himself into a lazy sitting position.

"That's not how I'd want to go." His inference was insulting. Did he think her shallow? Did he think money was all she cared about?

He adjusted his lean so his butt sat fully on a stair. "I know why you want to go. It's time I tell you why I want to stay."

"You already did." Though, she didn't like the way he made her caregiver duties sound vulgar.

"Not all of it." He paused, making her wait and wonder what he was going to reveal. The intensity in his eyes kept her speechless. "On the front lines, any little thump or snap or whisper could mean death. A good soldier," he hesitated, "I mean someone who stayed alive, had to be ready to react. Fire his weapon. Put on a gas mask. Charge the enemy. If not, your trench became your coffin." He adjusted his weight.

"You don't know what it's like living on the edge of death. My body needs time to recuperate from the front."

When she heard Geoff talk about war, she hated the Germans. She hated the killing and the scars. She hated all the scars. Even the ones she couldn't see.

She relaxed against the stair above. "It's noisy in Juneau."

"And when the Model-T backfired, I messed my bed. When Mrs. Prescott dropped a plate, I shook like a wet dog."

"I drop things."

He tilted his head back and laughed. "But here in the wilderness, I know it's just you. Just Jo being clumsy."

"You could replace me with someone sure-handed but..." She glanced down the staircase and shielded her eyes. "I don't see a line of women waiting to take my place."

Sighing, he said, "I don't think I'd survive breaking in someone else."

Scooting alongside Geoff, she took hold of his arm. "We can celebrate Christmas at the lodge. Maybe the goose will taste better than the one at Thanksgiving. I'll do my best not to drop it."

"Good. I finally won at something." Geoff sputtered a contented laugh. He slid, carefully, to the bottom stair.

She stood and placed her hands on her hips. "From now on the stairs are off limits. You're not Gregory."

"Thank heavens. I don't want to fight a bear."

In the afternoon, Josephine penned a letter to her mother explaining her absence at Christmas. She wrote that traveling and visitors would put a strain on Geoff's recovery. With her excuse complete, she read a letter from Ann.

Dear Josephine,

Marty Hill came to dinner on Sunday. He said you and Geoff Chambers visited the mine. He told me privately that you looked thin and pale, but Mr. Chambers looked quite robust. I trust this has nothing to do with the letter you wrote me regarding men. Do take care of yourself. Marty hopes to return soon.

I may hear as early as next week about the receptionist position at the bank. It doesn't pay much but think of all the men I'll meet.

Mother sends her love. Her new medicine seems to be easing her pain. She knitted a doily and...

Josephine couldn't finish the letter. Dread crept over her, the same dread that paralyzed her when Ivan approached. Did her sister think she was having relations with Geoff? Had Marty said something? Marty's gaze had touched her more intimately in one afternoon than Geoff's gaze had in months of care. She almost regretted writing about Greg and Daria. Almost. Seeing her story in a magazine was worth the gossip.

That night, before bed, she filled the tub and tested the water while Geoff lounged against the bathroom wall. His arms and chest were larger and more defined than the first time she attempted to help him bathe. Is this the robust look Marty had noticed?

When the water was the perfect temperature, she bent to lift Geoff's legs.

He held up a hand. "I've got this. Give me room."

"Let me help. It's my job." She'd blame her stupid Christmas tantrum if he fell.

"It's not about you." He pointed to his own chest and then motioned for her to move toward the doorway.

Humming a patriotic marching tune, he gripped the sides of the tub and lifted his stumps off the floor. His arm muscles bulged as he held the weight of his body upright. His butt crested the side of the tub and rested briefly on the rim. His left stump hurdled over the edge, but his right leg caught on the steel. His shoulders trembled with fatigue as he fought with his snagged stump.

"Let me do something." She reached for him.

"No," he snapped. "Stay back." He grunted his words.

Her fingernails embedded in her palms. *Please, God, no accidents.*

With red-faced determination, Geoff shifted the troublesome leg over the side of the tub. Dropping into the water, he exhaled with glee. He raised his hands into the air. "Wahoo! I did it."

She clapped for his success.

"Face the wall," he commanded, "and don't turn around."

She turned, grinning at his accomplishment.

Water sloshed in the tub. Suddenly, something hit the wall beside her.

She jumped.

His underwear slid to the ground leaving a wet streak on the wall.

"That is the last pair of drenched underwear you will have to deal with. From now on, I will bathe without clothes."

"You will?" She cleared her throat as she picked up the waterlogged shorts, still averting her gaze. "Can you get out of the tub on your own? Because I'm not giving this underwear back to you." She was teasingly serious.

"I don't know if I can hurl my wheelchair at a black bear, but I can lift myself out of this tub." He splashed in the water, filling the room with the fresh scent of soap.

His chipper whistling warmed her soul.

"I hope you like your early Christmas gift," he said. "No more bath duty."

"You mean if I had threatened to leave earlier, I could have gotten out of tub duty? I'll have to threaten you more often." Her laughter changed into a scream as water droplets drenched the back of her dress. She escaped from his shower with a smile on her face.

21

On December 24, 1918, she baked Geoff a birthday cake. Not chocolate, but strawberry. She didn't have any fresh berries, so she used strawberry flavored gelatin. The cake turned out more pink than red, but its mouth-watering aroma made the lodge smell like a bakery. With no food dye to darken the frosting for writing, she etched "21" on top of the cake with a toothpick.

Geoff glanced up from a pile of mining bills. "Can we have cake after lunch?"

"Think you'll be done with work by then?" She set the cake on the dining room table.

"I wish. Maybe the sugar will make my headache go away."

She retrieved a brown paper wrapped box from the kitchen. "Here's something that might ease your pain." She held out his gift.

"What's this?" He put down his papers. "You didn't have to get me anything."

Her hand stayed outstretched. "It's customary in my family to give someone a gift if you see them on their birthday. It's not expensive or fancy."

"I can't." He shifted his gaze to a ledger.

"Take it." She placed the box on his stump.

"You're the only one who will understand the meaning. I made your gift to pass the time. Nothing more."

He stared at the box. "I'll take it if you promise no more gifts."

"Only handmade," she said.

He unwrapped her gift slowly as if he was thinking of reconsidering her offer. Crunching up the paper, he tossed it onto the coffee table. Opening the flaps, he lifted out a pillow decorated with needlepoint cards. A king of hearts. A queen of hearts. A jack of hearts. And a ten of hearts.

"That's the first run I beat you with." She picked up the wad of paper. "A friendly reminder you haven't bested me in rummy."

He grinned. "One of these days, I'm going to beat you with this same hand. Thanks, Runt."

Grabbing her wool coat from the closet, she headed for the back door.

"Happy Birthday, Old Man."

Geoff propped his birthday pillow on the couch. "Where are you going? It's starting to snow."

"There's a four-foot fir near the path. It will make a perfect Christmas tree for the living room."

"We don't need to decorate."

"It's a tradition. My family cuts down a tree every Christmas Eve. And since…" She broke off her sentence. She didn't want to revisit the traveling argument.

"Then I'll come along. No sense in breaking tradition."

She stopped buttoning her coat. Was he feeling nostalgic, too?

"I'll need legs and my walking stick." He shifted

some papers, hesitated, then waved her on. "It's too much trouble. You could have the tree decorated before I'm ready to go."

"Are you bluffing? I'm an expert at those straps." She dashed into his room before he could change his mind and brought his wooden stilts. "Besides, the fresh air will do wonders for your head."

He removed his cut-off pants. "You sound like Doc Miller, Jr."

She held out his left leg. "If the shoe fits?"

"Hah. Funny." He was strapped and dressed in record time.

As they exited the back door, snow drifted slantwise across the landscape making it seem as if heaven was sprinkling white confetti over the lodge. Geoff gripped his walking stick in one hand and the rifle in the other. She carried an axe and a saw. All in all, they were well prepared and well armed.

"I'm not taking any chances." Geoff plunged his walking stick into the snow. "There was a black bear nosing around a day ago."

"Wonder if he likes strawberry cake?" She giggled. He frowned.

The beast trotted out from snow-dusted fronds.

Geoff pointed his stick at the dog. "I swear, if that animal knocks me over."

"You'll swear regardless if he knocks you down or not." She bent over and brushed snowflakes off her pet.

"No use drying him with your hand." Geoff balanced on his wooden staff and eyed the beast suspiciously. "He's going to get wet with this snow."

"We could bring him inside for the night." She held her breath hoping for agreement.

"Absolutely not. The porch is sufficient for a wild dog."

She stopped petting the canine and found the fir tree she had spotted previously. As the saw's teeth cut into the bark, the scent of evergreen wafted to her nose reminding her of carolers and candle lights.

"Now it smells like Christmas." She breathed deeply and continued with the saw. Back and forth. Back and forth. Her arm ached. Back and forth. Her arm burned. Back and forth. Fortunately, the fir collapsed onto the trail.

"Tim-ber," Geoff called like a seasoned lumberjack.

Grabbing the trunk, she dragged the tree through the snow with her non-sawing arm.

"Good thing it's not much bigger or it would be dragging you." He tried to match her pace. His wooden shoes packed the snow leaving a trail.

When they reached the porch, she handed him a hammer. "You can nail the planks on for a stand. I'll hold the tree. I already smell like pancake syrup."

"That's not the only thing you smell of." *Clink. Clink. Clink.*

"Wet dog?" She leaned in to sniff her hands.

"Summer garden." *Clink. Clink.* "I noticed your perfume in the house. I like it."

Heat flooded her face. His flattery made her feel as tall as the oldest pines. "I opened an early Christmas gift from my mom. She sent a sachet of sweet pea and gardenia."

He stood the tree on its stand. "It's nice."

The tree or her fragrance? She grabbed hold of the trunk and headed for the stairs. "What would be really nice is the scent of warm beast."

Geoff clutched the hammer in his hand like a weapon. "That's not on my Christmas list."

But it was on hers.

~*~

That night they sat by their little tree and opened greeting cards. She opened a card from her family. Her heart warmed at her mother's legible cursive. Her heart sunk to her toes when she read Ann had begun seeing Marty Hill. Would Geoff be upset if Marty spent more time in Juneau?

"Now here's a man that knows how to celebrate the holidays." Geoff held up a card from Brice Todd. "Tropical sun, beaches."

She glanced at Brice's opulent card and pictured his blond hair and bronzed body lying on the beach in nothing but shorts, not even sandals. Somehow, the image didn't entice her as much as it had when they were at the mansion.

"What are you thinking about?"

Her head jerked up. Envelopes fell off the arm of her chair.

"I was thinking about the beach," she stammered. "How nice it would be to be somewhere warm. I haven't been out of Alaska."

"I hadn't been out of the country until I enlisted." Geoff rested his arm on her needlepoint pillow. The fir tree looked as if it was growing out of his head.

Is that why he went to war? She placed her family's Christmas card on the table. Her damp palms had curled the edges.

"Why did you go to war?" She licked her parched lips.

Geoff stopped organizing cards. Glittering ornaments on the top card held his interest.

Oh, why did she blurt that out? "I shouldn't pry." She rocked forward. "More tea?"

"No. No tea." He manipulated his stumps so he sat higher against the back of the couch. "It's not a horrible secret why I fought. Although, no one brings it up anymore. I met a need." He glanced at her. "Somewhat like you."

"Being a caregiver is different than being a soldier. I barely left home." She finished off a few drops of cold tea. "And our fights aren't to the death." She gave a stiff nod to his pressed-lipped grin. She didn't want to be reminded of her mistakes.

"I read of a need for engineers in Europe." His index finger rotated round and round and round on the arm rest. "I have no formal degree but practically growing up at Kat Wil, I'd seen plenty of land surveys. Ask me to build a sluice. Done. Beam a tunnel. No problem. Reinforce a trench. Easy." His fingernail picked at the leather. "I wasn't supposed to be first defense. But trench lines change. You think a section is British and it spews out Germans."

"It doesn't sound very organized."

His gaze bore through her. "It's not when men are dying."

She shifted to the edge of her seat. "I'm thankful it's over."

"Over?" He slapped his mutilated thigh. "I thought I'd come back alive. A bit of shrapnel embedded in my skin maybe. Or in a coffin. I never imagined this." He drew a hand across his uneven legs.

Her conscience ached for all the times she'd cursed Geoff, cursed his foul moods, cursed the work involved in his care. Why hadn't she tried to understand his war wounds earlier?

Reaching out, she grabbed hold of the arm rest on the couch. "I'm sure your family was proud of you." *I'm proud.*

"It was my decision. My father supported it." He glanced at a Christmas card from his family. "My father has Bradley. Brice's father wouldn't permit him to go to war. Brice is his only son."

Had Brice visited the Chamberses' mansion that day because he felt guilty that his best friend was an amputee? Is a friend losing his life easier than a friend losing his dignity? She was determined all the more to see Geoff overcome his injuries.

"Did I depress you, Runt?" He shifted closer.

She shook her head. "And if I was sad, it would be my own fault for bringing up the war." A war she didn't understand. Europe seemed so far away from Juneau. She had been bitter and selfish about this job. Bitter about relocating to the lodge. Selfish for resenting the care he required. That needed to change.

He continued to stare.

She popped out of the chair. "I'd like some tea."

"At this hour? You?" He clapped his hands. "Great. You'll be alert for a game of birthday rummy."

"If you birthday wished for a win, you're in trouble."

~*~

At midnight, the invisible soldiers returned to torment Geoff. At least they had waited until his birthday had ended. Grabbing a blanket and the afghan, she hurried to his room.

"Geoff," she whispered. She wanted to be sure he was awake, aware, and not aggressive.

"Jo," he said breathily. "I had a nightmare."

"Must have been all our trench talk." She checked his forehead. Clammy but cool.

"Will you stay with me?"

She held up the white covering. "I brought the afghan, so I could curl up on the couch."

"Curl up at my feet so I know you're near."

Was he slipping into another memory? He didn't have feet.

He sat against the head board. "What time is it?"

"Almost two in the morning." She lay on her side, on the bed, facing him.

He sank back into his pillow. "Merry Christmas, Jo."

Wrapping the afghan around her body, she said, "Merry Christmas, outstanding veteran."

Her veteran.

22

The new year—1919—came. She remained the Gin Rummy queen. As she crossed the days off her calendar, she willed the sound of yipping dogs to break the silence and bring her a copy of February's *Woman's Home Companion.*

A faint shouting echoed in the tall spruce.

"Your boyfriend's back," Geoff called.

She shut the oven door and then dressed in a coat and boots in record time. Stuffing her hair in a woven cap, she sprinted to the porch.

The Aleutian musher held out a sack of mail.

"Won't you stay and have some tea with us?" she asked.

"No stopping," the musher mumbled.

She hurried into the lodge, handed Geoff the mail, shoved her coat in the closet, and stationed herself next to Geoff's spot on the couch. Hovering over his shoulder, she scanned each letter as he flipped through the mail.

"Belated birthday cards for me." Geoff flung his cards onto the next cushion. "Two letters for you." He held up an envelope. *"Woman's Home Companion,* editorial office."

She whisked the letter out of his hand.

"Open it down here. I'm not allowed to chase you upstairs. Besides, your typist deserves some consideration."

Sliding her finger under the lip of the envelope, she removed the letter and sped through the first paragraph—greetings and a commendation for entering the contest. She concentrated on every word in the second paragraph. Her heart stuttered. The story winner was—Mr. Morris Hennessey of Scranton, Pennsylvania.

She read his name again and again as if the lettering would morph and change and proclaim her the victor.

"Well," Geoff prompted.

She folded the letter and smoothed the crease between her fingers. An odd buzzing hummed in her ears.

"I didn't win." *I let you down.* "They picked a man from Pennsylvania." Her eyelids fluttered. "*Outcast* sounds like an interesting story."

"Outcast?" His voice rose with disbelief. "How could you get more outcast than an amputee on an Alaskan island?"

She picked up her other letters from the table. "It was my first try at writing. Guess I wasn't good enough."

"Your story was first-rate." His affirmation was awkwardly high-pitched. "They played it safe. Didn't want to draw a wheelchair, or a cut-off man. I should have let you write a fairy tale." He wadded up the mail sack and threw it in the fire.

His praise dulled the sting of losing. "I wouldn't have written my story any other way."

"Well, I'm proud of Greg and Daria. In fact, I'm making flapjacks for dinner to treat the best darn writer I know." He tugged on the arm of his wheelchair to bring it closer.

"You don't know many writers, do you?" She tried to smile but found it broken. "And I don't mind cooking dinner. It's something I'm good at. Bet I'm better than Mr. Hennessey."

She halted in the threshold of the kitchen. "You might want to sneak in a game of cards tonight, seems like my luck's changing."

Later, she sat on her bed and opened mail, hoping for happier news. The scent of crushed roses filled her nostrils. A letter from Ann rested on top of the pile. She read her sister's news.

Marty proposed!

What! Her stomach twisted like discarded thread. She read on.

We intend to wed this summer. Mother is checking dates with Father Demetriev. I couldn't be happier. Marty is so handsome in his three-piece suit.

Please do not mention the engagement to Mr. Chambers. Marty doesn't want him worrying about the mine.

Hah! Marty doesn't want Geoff worrying about those crooked ledgers, the gambling, and the mysterious Mr. Young. She crumpled the letter and threw it in the corner of the room.

Worst. Day. Ever.

She flopped backward on the bed. Mr. Hennessey was probably celebrating his victory, brimming with satisfaction at seeing his story in print. In a little over four months, she would be home sewing dresses. First and foremost would be Ann's wedding dress. She should be happy for her sister. If anyone could keep Marty Hill tightly stitched and straight ironed, it was headstrong Ann.

Rolling on her side, her chest hiccupped. It sank and rose and sank even deeper.

Tears followed.

Why did she write that story? Did people even care about Geoff's sacrifice? Or was it easier to pretend veterans like Geoff didn't exist? She had let Geoff down. But she would make sure he had the best possible care in their last few months together.

That night, she tallied the rummy wins:

Geoff- 18

Jo- 7

Darn. Her luck had changed.

~*~

Two weeks later, she was bent over the tub, her hands covered in cleanser, when she heard a strange clicking sound as if Geoff had borrowed her heeled boots. She sat back and shook the hair out of her eyes. Geoff wearing shoes? Impossible. Washing the cleanser from her hands, she went to investigate.

In the middle of the living room, Geoff and the beast were in a tug-of-war over a bright red bandanna.

"What is going on in here?"

Geoff pushed on the beast's hind quarters.

"Sit, dog, sit."

The beast released the bandanna and jogged her direction. He sat at attention, dusting the floor with his tail. She bent over and rubbed his cool snout.

"Oh, come on. We practiced, you traitor." Geoff walked stiff-legged to the couch. "What do you say?

Do I get a smile? I captured that mutt and let him in my house. It's been too quiet around here. I'm tired of winning at cards. It's more enjoyable trying to beat you."

The beast barked at Geoff's exasperated rant.

She turned toward Geoff and tried to keep a straight face, but laughter rang out of her mouth.

"That was the most ridiculous tug-of-war I have ever seen."

"I thought he'd play nice." Geoff crossed his arms and fake pouted.

Rubbing the beast's ears, she said, "I have been a bit down, but don't worry. I'm going to pump up that Singer machine and sew. Crafting patterns will help me forget about the contest."

"Good. Because if Tubby sees puffy eyes and a forlorn face, I'll get the blame."

"Tubby won't be out this way for a while."

"Since the winter's been mild, I'm thinking he might be able to ferry out in March."

"Ferry?"

"Our families." Geoff reached over and gestured for the beast to come near. When the dog did, Geoff yanked the bandanna from the beast's mouth. A triumphant grin lit up his face. "We'll invite everyone out to the lodge."

Everyone?

23

"Both our families?" The beast cocked his head at her squeak of a question.

"Yes, your family and mine. My father, Bradley… I doubt Julia will come."

She didn't answer. A surge of energy had her mind racing with a list of tasks that needed to be done.

"Well, say something. I can't read that darn poker face of yours."

"You really mean it?" She grasped the back of her chair to steady herself.

"Yes. You give me absolutely no hint of what you're thinking." He tossed the handkerchief up in the air and watched it float to the floor.

"No." She chuckled. "I mean the party. We'll host it here?"

"Why not? We need some fun. Bradley's been eager to come for a visit. Since you didn't go home at Christmas, you can catch up with your family."

She would see her mother. Hear the town gossip. She jumped over the dog and flung her arms around Geoff's neck. His hands steadied her weight.

"Thank you." Her words came out muffled against his shoulder. He smelled of soap and damp dog fur. She pulled from his embrace. "I know you don't like company, but my mother will be able to see where we live."

Geoff still gripped her body. Her heart pumped a fast beat. His firm touch made her want to hug him one more time.

She didn't.

Instead, she reclined in her chair with her feet tucked underneath her skirt. The beast nuzzled her arm looking for affection.

"My mother will be able to picture where I am when she reads my letters."

"I thought you'd like this idea. I'll notify Tubby to put us on the schedule."

"If we're going to host our families, we'll need to decorate the lodge." She scanned the living room making mental notes of improvements.

"What's wrong with the lodge?" He lounged on the couch as if the beast had tired him out. "Looks fine to me."

She tilted her head. "There are no colorful pillows to accent this room or your bed. The sheers are tattered on the bottom…"

"Jo, it's a party. No one will care about pillows."

"The window treatments are front and center for everyone to see. That'll be my first project."

"Project? Sounds like work. I want us to have fun." He combed his fingers through his hair. Did he regret mentioning the party?

"Oh, we will have fun. But first, I need to order material and pick out colors. We'll need a new tablecloth, too."

"Colors?" He repeated as if he'd never heard the word.

"Don't worry. I'll use blues and greens—manly

hues. Right, boy?" She smoothed the beast's ruff. "Oh, um." Her mouth became as dry as talcum powder. The money she had at the lodge wouldn't cover but a few yards of fabric. "Can I order material? With your money?"

He rubbed his chin looking as if he was deep in thought.

It was a simple question. What did he have to ponder?

His eyebrows arched and a grin as wide as her enthusiasm flashed across his face. "Order whatever *you* need."

~*~

On Saturday, March 22, she dashed to Geoff's bedroom and arranged clothes, legs, and decorative pillows.

"Slow down." Geoff ate a bite of egg. "I haven't seen you this crazy. You're going to be exhausted before the ship docks."

She poked her head into the dining room. "We haven't hosted a party before. I want everything to be spit-polish perfect."

"Look outside. It's a glorious forty-nine degrees and no snow or rain. We're hosting our families and a captain who, even if you served burned wieners and beans, would say he never tasted better. Besides, the ginger snaps you baked yesterday are the best you've ever made."

"You ate one?"

"Two, but there are plenty left. I would have snitched a piece of pie, but I didn't want to incur your wrath. Remember, this is supposed to be fun."

A weary smile crossed her face. "You're right."

"Most of the time," he added.

Shaking her head, she said, "Please go get dressed." She wished he were more mobile and more able to assist her. "I don't want to be strapping on legs at the last minute."

"I've mastered those wooden legs." He slid into his wheelchair. "You're only needed if there's an alignment problem."

She raced up the stairs the moment his bedroom door closed. She adorned her taupe dress with a navy voile vest—a pattern from last month's *Companion*. Braiding her hair, she fastened it in a bun, leaving ringlets to frame her face. Deep breaths, she told herself, while fanning her face with her fingers.

A tapping noise sounded from the bottom of the stairs.

She peeked from her bedroom door and descended the steps.

Geoff stood on the lower landing, looking tall, handsome and regal.

"New dress?" he asked.

"New vest." She gripped the handrail to steady her wobbly ankles. "The color's not too bold, is it?"

"Turn around." He gestured with his hand.

She obliged, turning slowly on the bottom step.

"Works for me. It has a nice hand rest in the back."

"That's an embellishment, not a handrail. You've been walking fine the last couple of weeks."

He grinned as if her praise was a freshly baked ginger snap.

Time dragged. She paced from the front bay window to the kitchen. Why couldn't the guest list include only her mother and Ann?

When Geoff announced the ship's arrival in the inlet, she dried her palms on a dish rag. She practiced a hostess smile and hoped guests didn't notice the quiver in her lips.

Together, she and Geoff stood on the porch and watched Tubby dock the *Maiden.*

"Who's that man with my father?" Geoff asked. His head bobbed as he tried to get a better view of the visitor.

She squinted, straining to make out the gentleman's face. "It's Marty Hill. Your manager."

Geoff swore. His jaw tightened. "Bet he wishes my body disintegrated on the banks of the Marne."

"Surely not." Her sister thought Marty was marriage material. Marty was hospitable enough at the mine.

"Who invited him?" Geoff emphasized the last word as if Marty came with a case of diphtheria.

This was not the time to mention her sister's engagement. Ann might have invited Marty. She hoped it had been Mr. Chambers or Tubby. She shrugged and said, "I don't know."

Geoff's walking stick berated the porch. *Thamp. Thamp. Thamp.*

"Guess we should move out." His hand rested on her shoulder as he shadowed her body to the dock.

The first one off the *Maiden* was Bradley. The boy jumped ship before it was secured. Bradley bounded up the length of the dock, making a beeline for his brother.

Her vest tightened mid-back.

"Don't let me go down," Geoff whispered.

Immediately, she flung open her arms as if expecting an embrace. "Bradley," she called as if they had been lifelong friends. A leather case bounced off the boy's hip. "What did you bring us?"

Bradley stopped short of bowling over his brother. He opened the case and displayed a camera.

"Mother bought me a Kodak autographic in San Francisco." His fingers unlatched and expanded the camera like an expert. "I'm going to take pictures of everyone at the lodge."

One disaster averted.

Geoff let go of her vest and lauded Bradley's gift.

"Wonderful," she said.

"Bradley, put that camera away 'til later," Mr. Chambers called from the gangplank. The elder Chambers carefully escorted his wife down each step. Julia Chambers's gloved hand bobbed elegantly in the air as she balanced on her husband's arm.

Josephine studied the plum-colored satin dress emerging from the hem of Mrs. Chambers's coat. Deep purple cloth was expensive, and Josephine had never created a dress in such a rare color. Mrs. Chambers must have found another seamstress.

Josephine shook the sadness from her heart. Mrs. Chambers had no reason to wait for summer to purchase a new gown.

Geoff planted his stick in the ground a few feet from the dock.

Bradley grabbed hold of the stick, imitating his big brother. Josephine wished she had her own camera to capture the two brothers, side by side.

"I can't believe she came," Geoff breathed into her ear.

"We have a few surprise guests." She looked up and met Geoff's gaze. "Should be an interesting afternoon."

"What have you done to my son?" Mr. Chambers said. He inspected Geoff from the black shoes to the hat-brimmed head. "I didn't expect you to be walking. Tall and..." Mr. Chambers's lips pressed together. His eyes glistened as he ruffled Bradley's hair.

"Handsome." Julia finished her husband's sentence. She leaned forward to kiss Geoff's cheek, catching more air than skin. The scent of blooming lilies filled the air. "And Josephine," she added, turning her attention from Geoff, "You've outdone yourself. That vest is exquisite. You must design me one when you're back in town."

"I'd ask for one, but she insists I wear pinstripes," Geoff joked. The laughter calmed Josephine's nerves.

Marty and Ann sauntered toward the gathering. Geoff released his hold on Josephine's back and shook his father's hand.

Mr. Chambers cleared his throat. "Miss Josephine, you've met Mr. Hill, our manager."

"She's actually driven with him and survived," Ann remarked. Laughter erupted again.

"Don't tell stories, dear." Marty gave Ann's arm a quick caress.

From the corner of her eye, she noticed Geoff look her direction. She did not acknowledge him. Ann had sworn her to secrecy. Geoff would have to figure Ann and Marty's relationship out on his own. By the end of the afternoon, Marty would have to fess up. Ann would have to fess up. Or she would slip her mother some of Geoff's "medicinal party wine," and her mother would fess up.

Her mother waddled up the dock, clinging to Tubby's sturdy arm.

"Excuse me." Josephine hurried to help Tubby

with her mother. A swell of emotion made every breath a struggle.

Her mother tried to hasten her gait. Her upper-half was willing, but her arthritic toes rebelled.

"Where is my baby," her mother gasped. "Josephine Primrose, you are a salve for my heart."

Josephine embraced her mother. "I'm happy you're here. I have missed our talks."

Her mother's eyes brightened. "The lodge is bigger than I imagined, and Master Chambers does seem healthy."

"Geoff Chambers gets around very well when he puts his mind to it." Josephine sneaked another hug.

By the time she, Tubby, and her mother reached the porch, Geoff and the other guests were milling around the living room. She rushed inside to take coats and hats and arrange another place setting at the table. Two crewmen carrying a large vertical crate bumped open the door.

Conversation stopped.

"Where would you like this Victrola, Cap'n?" a crew member asked.

"I didn't order a record player." Geoff seemed amused. "My dancing days are over."

"It's a house warming present." Mr. Chambers settled an arm across his son's shoulders. "I thought we might like some music with dinner. This island could use a little light opera." Mr. Chambers indicated the vacant corner in the dining room where Geoff did his push-ups. "You've space right over there."

"What a lovely gift." Josephine gave Geoff a stern look not to contradict her. She admired the mahogany Victrola. The carved legs and pull-handle doors were similar to the one she had seen at the Chamberses' mansion. Advertisements in the *Companion* priced the record players at four hundred dollars.

Bradley opened a leather satchel. "We brought records, too." The excitement in his voice rivaled a gift exchange on Christmas morning.

"Perhaps you could start us off with a favorite song," she encouraged Bradley so he would have fun in a room full of adults.

Julia supervised Bradley's choice. "Geraldine Ferrar would be splendid."

The crackling drag of the needle soon brought to life the soprano's soothing song.

Geoff and his father inspected the wines while she tended to dinner. Marty offered to carve the roast, and since Geoff was busy in the dining room, she accepted his offer. Ann arranged the roast, potatoes, and green beans on the plates. Gravy and rolls would be passed. Ann was quite the assistant. Would she have been as helpful if Marty had not been in close proximity?

Geoff gave a *tink, tink, tink* to his glass, calling everyone to the table. She took the open seat next to Geoff, across from her mother. Ann sat across from Marty Hill. Julia sat across from Mr. Chambers. Tubby and Bradley shared the end of the table.

After Geoff gave the blessing, Mr. Chambers raised his glass.

"A toast." He looked toward his oldest son. "To our veterans, to peace, and to President Wilson."

Glasses clinked. Voices chorused their approval.

Josephine touched the wine glass to her lips and inhaled the heavy grape aroma. She did not taste one drop.

"Have you seen any ghosts?" Bradley's question halted the clanging of silverware.

Tubby gave a hearty sailor's laugh and clapped Bradley on the shoulder.

"Can't say I've seen a flicker of Old Man Gilbertsen."

"Perhaps once." Josephine chimed in the conversation before Mr. Chambers could reprimand Bradley for poor table manners. "Shortly after we moved in, your brother called out, thinking he had seen a white wisp in his room."

"It was tiny," Geoff interrupted. "Probably just a flash of light. If it was a ghost, it was the runt of the litter." He grinned at Josephine. "Now, our dog scares away any intruders."

She tilted her head. "Our dog?"

"Don't tell me you've forgotten our pet, Riley?" He tipped his goblet toward her before taking a sip. "Named after the Vice President. Thomas Riley Marshall."

"Oh yes, Riley." She tipped her glass back toward Geoff. "He guards our huckleberry bushes."

Tubby's gaze darted between her and Geoff. He wiped his whiskers with a napkin.

"Franklin Gilbertsen didn't die here, son." Tubby leaned back in his chair as if to tell a seaman's yarn. He pointed to the staircase. "Tumbled right down those stairs. Snapped his leg bone like a twig. His—"

"Pneumonia's what took him, Captain." Her mother raised a goblet, saving the table from gruesome details. "Josephine helped comfort Mr. Gilbertsen during his last days. The only reason Mr. Gilbertsen would show up here is to say thank you."

"It's a good thing Widow Gilbertsen sold the lodge." Ann turned to Josephine. "She hardly leaves the house anymore. Last time I dropped by she inquired when you would be back in town."

"Well, not for a while." Josephine flashed a glorious smile. "I'm here on the island until June. Remember?"

Ann stared at Geoff. Was she trying to gage his reaction? Geoff poured gravy on his roast and acted as if the conversation didn't concern him. No drips. No eye contact. Nothing. She passed the rolls to Mr. Hill.

"What do you do here for fun?" Bradley asked, addressing his brother from the other end of the table.

All eyes focused on Geoff.

Geoff cleared his throat. "We read magazines, write letters, do work. I've taught Josephine how to—"

Her eyes widened in horror. *Don't say gin or rummy or cards.*

Geoff must have noticed her face. "Uh," he stammered. "We tally ledgers."

"Yes, I'll need spectacles by summer." She squinted and crinkled her nose, inspecting the tablecloth.

Everyone laughed.

Lively conversation filled the table—labor strikes, the Versailles Treaty, salmon marinade. After the last piece of Alaskan blueberry pie was served, Josephine sat down, tea in hand.

"May I take your picture after pie, Miss Josephine?" Bradley asked.

How could she resist the boy's excited smile? "Sure, as long as my teeth aren't purple."

Bradley jumped from his seat and excused himself to prepare his camera.

Marty Hill stabbed at a piece of pie crust with his fork. Josephine hated to see a guest bored.

She leaned toward Marty. "There's a path that

leads to a waterfall. It's probably a trickling icicle now, but I'd love for Ann to see it. It would be treacherous for mother to attempt the walk."

"Say no more," Marty said. "It would be my privilege to accompany Ann."

Ann accepted the offer with a sultry wink.

After dessert, Mr. and Mrs. Chambers, Geoff, and Bradley headed out front for family pictures. Tubby and her mother settled on the porch. The musky, sweet scent of the captain's tobacco wafted through the front door as Josephine cleared the dishes.

After piling the last of the plates into the sink, she whipped around and almost plowed into Marty Hill.

"Mr. Hill, forgive me. I didn't expect anyone to be in the kitchen."

"Please, call me Marty. Mr. Hill is my father. Makes me feel old." She expected the man to step backward and give her some room, but he stood his ground, pinning her against the sink. "I came to compliment you on dinner. Best meal I've had in a long time."

"Thank you." Her gaze shifted between her clasped hands and Marty's face. When he exhaled, she felt a breeze of air on her forehead.

"You've worked a miracle with Geoff Chambers. I haven't seen him in such fine spirits. What did you give him? A special tonic?"

She smiled weakly at his flattery and averted her gaze. Geoff wasn't fond of Marty, but it wasn't her place to meddle in mine business.

"Good food and rest is what the doctor ordered." Her eyes danced from Marty to the doorway, hoping her sister would sweep Marty away so she could get back to the dishes and ultimately her guests.

"This lodge is not far from Kat Wil. You could come back to the mine for another tour. On your day off perhaps?"

The inflection in Marty's voice suggested he had more to offer than a tour. Did he believe the crude insults his miners cast? Her mouth gaped. He was engaged. Engaged to her sister.

Shifting down the counter, she sputtered a refusal.

"Hill." Geoff's voice rang out from the doorway. His tone reminded her of his morphine-demanding rants.

Marty spun around.

She slumped against the counter.

"Josephine is needed for pictures. Ann is waiting by the path. And…" Geoff fixed a glare on his manager that had her own heart trembling in fear, "my nurse accompanies me to my mine. Remember that."

Marty took a step backward—onto her toes.

She clenched her teeth and vice-gripped the counter.

"Of course," Marty said as if they had been discussing improvements at Kat Wil. With a nod in her direction, he fled from the kitchen without an apology for stomping on her foot.

"Bradley's waiting." Geoff's piercing glare rattled her composure more than Marty's pass.

Smoothing a few strands of hair behind her ear, she glanced at the sink. All she had been doing was the dishes. Did Geoff think she had been flirting with his manager?

She stepped toward Geoff. "Would you like my shoulder?"

He turned and balanced on his walking stick. "I've got this down."

In silence, she followed him through the living room and out the front door.

Bradley waited near the dock with his camera.

"I hope my teeth aren't blue?" Her face brightened into a toothy smile.

"I can't see." Bradley waved them closer. "Stand next to my brother so I can get a picture of you and the lodge. I've taken everyone else."

She inched closer to Geoff. Side by side they stood, staring at the lens of the camera.

"Wait," she shouted. She ran toward a pile of crates stacked on the dock and chose the sturdiest. She placed it on the ground next to Geoff.

"Cheater," Geoff whispered.

"The picture will look lopsided now that you're taller." She grinned and stretched closer to his height. "Besides, aren't you cheating a bit?"

"On three." Bradley adjusted the lens. "One, two..."

Geoff's fingers slipped under her vest and tickled her waist.

Her gaze darted upward, meeting his.

"Three."

The shutter clicked.

"Can we take another one, Bradley?" She poked Geoff's chest. "No shenanigans this time."

Geoff grinned wider than the inlet. "Whatever do you mean? I'm helping you smile for the photograph. This is a party, isn't it?"

Had she ever seen him this lighthearted before? Maybe when he won at cards?

She readied for another picture.

"Say Riley," Bradley yelled.

"Guess we have an inside dog," she mused.

~*~

By afternoon, she had conversed more than she had since arriving at the lodge. Julia wanted her opinion on hats and dress lengths. Her mother spoke of neighbors and new medicines. Tubby spoke of evading the influenza on his travels. Geoff, Mr. Chambers, and Marty talked about the mine. Bradley threw a stick for Riley, the newly named beast, to retrieve.

"Here, boy. Here, Riley." The dog dropped the branch at Bradley's feet.

Yep, the name Riley is here to stay. From beast to pet.

Shortly after tea, Ann pulled her into Geoff's bedroom.

"When were you going to tell me?" Ann threw her hands up in the air. "I wrote you about my Marty."

Josephine's stomach swirled like an eddy. Did Geoff tell Ann about Marty's invitation to the mine? Did Marty confess? Not likely. She sighed not wanting the party to end on an off-key note.

"I didn't think it was my place to say anything." Josephine's muscles tensed in anticipation of one of Ann's tirades.

"When is Geoff going to make the announcement? We're all waiting for the big news." Ann crossed her arms and cinched them against her waist.

"Announcement?" Josephine crinkled her nose in confusion. "What announcement? This is a family gathering."

Ann playfully swatted her arm. "The announcement about your engagement, silly."

24

"Engagement?" Josephine repeated in a raspy whisper. Was this a joke? "How on earth did—?"

"I knew a man and a woman alone in the woods could never come to any good." Ann giggled. "Mistakenly, I assumed Geoff's injuries were more severe."

"Oh. No." Josephine tried to correct her sister.

"It was only a matter of time, really. Marty told me his hands were all over you when you visited the mine. Who can blame the man?" Ann reached out and cupped Josephine's breasts. "You've got curves."

"Stop it." Josephine removed her sister's hands. "Geoff and I have not been—" She didn't know how to phrase it. "We're not—"

"So, you're going to wait?" Ann's face grew serious. "Is it because?" Her sister mimicked a saw going across her thighs.

"No." Josephine gasped. "Geoff and I are not getting married. I don't know why you thought we were."

"You're serious?" Ann cocked her head. "There's not going to be a wedding?"

"Honestly, I don't know where you got the idea."

"Oh, come now." Ann flicked her hand so

abruptly Josephine had to step back to miss getting scratched. "Both families are summoned to the lodge." Ann pointed her finger at the wall to the living room. "Julia Chambers is here. Royalty makes more appearances than that woman. And the Victrola?" Ann's voice actually squawked. "If that's not an engagement gift, what is?"

"It's a housewarming gift." Josephine's heart jumped into her throat. Did others think the same thing as her sister?

"Precisely. This is not your house. It's his. And isn't he leaving come June?"

Josephine's pulse throbbed in her temples. She was sure her face was flushed crimson. "I'm sorry if you misunderstood." Big breath. "I am Geoff's caregiver. Nothing more." Hearing her own business-like description of her role nagged at her heart. "I was feeling down and a little homesick. I had entered a writing contest in the *Companion* and lost. Geoff was trying to cheer me up by throwing this party."

"You wrote a story for a magazine?" Ann snorted. "Why, that's more preposterous than bedding a cripple. Although with his money, one could try and turn a blind eye." Ann shook her head. "Silly Josephine, skilled writers can't get published in the *Companion*. And you barely finished grade eight."

Josephine's shoulders dipped as if Geoff had just taken hold.

"Mother doesn't believe I'm getting married, does she?"

"She hasn't mentioned it to me. But then I've been discreet. I don't share Marty's whisperings with her."

Ann stepped forward almost pinning her to the wall. The repeated poke of her sister's finger was like a surging needle.

"Your job is to keep Geoff Chambers healthy. Story writing and pouting about it will only get you fired." Ann straightened her dress. Flipping her hair, she gave Josephine a stern once over. "I will not take on another job to support this family. I must be available when Marty needs me. No more writing. Do you hear?"

She nodded, fearing her sister would not move until she did.

"Good. Now, you have guests to attend to. And I, as one, need another glass of Chardonnay."

Ann swung open the bedroom door and vanished into the living room.

Blood pulsed into Josephine's cheeks. Pressure built behind her eyes. She would not release the tears. She had met Geoff's needs and written a serial without any help from her sister. Ann had no right to tell her how to do her job.

Perfecting her posture, she released a calming breath and smiled wide like the perfect hostess should. An up-tempo tuba and brass selection from the Victrola greeted her as she stepped into the living room.

Bradley grinned at his parents. The boy held up a miniature walking stick not quite a third the size of Geoff's. He moved the tapered branch up and down like a baton. Ann, Marty, and her mother sat at the dining table, a bottle of wine centered between them. Tubby's cherry-scented pipe smoke hung in the room.

"It's about time we get aboard." The captain's hand waved everyone toward the door. "Been a full day."

Full of surprises.

"Captain," Josephine began, "next time you must bring your wife. I would like to meet her."

Tubby held her gaze longer than he ever had. "I'd never get her out of here if she saw you." With a wink, he turned and rallied the party goers to make their way to his ship.

What did Tubby mean about his wife? She didn't have time to follow up. She had to see her guests to the dock. Geoff walked on his own with his balancing stick. Bradley matched him hole for hole with his newly discovered branch.

"No writing for three months," Ann warned, giving her a stiff-armed hug before practically pushing Marty on board the boat.

Mr. Chambers embraced his son and then engulfed her in a wrestler's hug.

"Thank you," the patriarch whispered, "Geoff looks better than I imagined he ever could. I didn't think I would see my son again."

She hoped Mr. Chambers was remarking on Geoff's improving health—mental and physical—and not on her abilities as a caregiver.

"Geoff has come a long way," she said. "I can't take all the praise. He is very determined."

"Like his father." Julia motioned for Bradley and Geoff to join them. "Perhaps you'd enjoy a trip down the coast," she said to Geoff. "The influenza seems to have run its course. The warmth will do us all some good."

Josephine caught the meaning of "all." It meant the Chambers family. A family she didn't belong to even though she had spent more time with Geoff than his stepmother had since his return from the front. Julia had been her best customer and benefactor. Still, her stomach hollowed at the thought that all her hard work had been an expense on the monetary books.

"I'm not much on traveling," Geoff said.

Bradley tugged on his pant leg. "We're doing this again soon. Right?" Bradley asked as he threw a piece of driftwood to Riley.

"Anytime." Josephine glanced at the lodge. It was a nice home. But as Ann reminded her, it was not her home. It remained Geoff's temporary home.

Her mother was the last one aboard.

"You're a young woman, Josephine. I hate that you're growing up without me or your sister." Her mother stroked the length of Josephine's hair. The caress of her scalp reminded her of the injury Ivan had given here, but no pain radiated down her skull. "You do like it here, don't you?"

Tears sizzled behind Josephine's eyes. "Yes, it's a big house. I should make it a few more months." Her voice thinned to a wisp. "I do miss you."

Her mother cradled Josephine's face in her hands. "You make me proud. So very proud."

She would never tell her mother what she had endured for their family. Her fears and mistakes were better left untold. Some secrets should stay on Douglas Island.

Geoff waved good-bye from the dock. She stood by his side.

Tubby suddenly disembarked, huffing through pipe-gritting teeth.

"Your mail," Tubby said. "That magazine you like came a few weeks ago, Jo." He handed her March's *Companion.* Late, of course.

Mr. Hennessey's dream-crushing story would be inside.

"There's a letter for you, too. Is your subscription due?" Tubby held up an envelope.

Adrenaline surged through her body. She didn't have a subscription to the *Companion*. Geoff did. Her eyes focused on the return address—*Woman's Home Companion*, editorial office.

25

Josephine clutched the envelope and magazine to her chest, waiting until the *Maiden* disappeared before reading them.

Geoff jostled her up and down. "That was one of the best days ever. Thank you, Runt."

She didn't know if it was the emotional good-bye with her mother, the letter from the editorial office, or the dizzy feeling from being flung around like a rag doll, but as her vest dragged against Geoff, she felt lighter than a sea breeze. She couldn't blame the wine for this delightfully woozy sensation.

"Aren't you going to open it?" Geoff stepped away giving her room. "And don't tell me it's nothing. I haven't seen your eyes pop like that since you flattened me in the tub."

"I didn't…" It was no use defending her actions again. "It's probably nothing." She quick-stepped to the lodge.

Geoff gave chase.

She ripped open the envelope, flung it on her chair, and scanned the letter. Excitement exploded inside of her.

"Tell me." Geoff swept a hand through his wind-tossed hair.

"They want to print my story. Greg and Daria. The whole thing." She squealed like a mouse.

"But I thought the guy in Pennsylvania won?"

"He did, but they liked mine, too. Especially, since I take care of someone like Greg."

"How did they know that?" His congratulatory smile faded.

She nervously creased the folds of the letter. "On the entry form. My occupation. I listed that I'm a caregiver to a veteran. They want to run my story in June and July with the article running in May."

"Article? What article?" Geoff leaned on his walking stick.

"They've asked me to write about what it's like taking care of a veteran."

"A cripple."

"Someone injured in the war." She offered him a look at the letter.

He declined.

"I'm sharing what I've learned with others. And they'll pay me thirty dollars."

Geoff stroked his cleft chin. "I've got to make another trip to the mine. Look over surveys. I don't have time to type."

"But I can write the article, can't I?"

"I won't be much help. Tubby's returning Wednesday to take me out to Kat Wil."

The low burning fire crackled in the hearth. She wished a record played on the Victrola something upbeat and melodic to boost her confidence. The article was supposed to be about real life. Her real life. Geoff's real life. Their life together. She didn't know how much to reveal about bedsores, nightmares, walking lessons, and withdrawal?

"Jo."

She looked up to see him staring down at her.

"Write it. If not for me, then for all the men stuck in hospitals."

"You don't mind?"

He shook his head. "Right now, all I care about is getting in my chair. These wooden stumps have worn out their welcome."

"They'd like a picture of us." She took hold of his arm and helped him to his room. "I was thinking we could send one of Bradley's. The one of us together with the lodge in the background."

He cocked his head. "You didn't mention my picture would be sent all over the country."

"You do have an accomplished tailor and photographer." She stood at attention and saluted him. "We'll make sure you look mighty fine."

"I'll make sure we get the picture." He pinched the back of her vest. "I'm proud of you, Jo. Not many eighteen-year-olds can brag about having a serial published in a national magazine."

"I couldn't have done it without you."

"Sure, you could. Greg would be a Leonard with long tapered legs."

She laughed, relieved he had taken the news so well. "Would you mind if I didn't accompany you to the mine? With the delay in getting the mail, I only have a few weeks to finish."

"What? And not see your future brother-in-law?" He wiggled his eyebrows.

"You know?" *I should have told him.*

"Marty confessed," he added. "We serve excellent wine. Too bad you don't imbibe, or I would have found out sooner."

She cleared her throat. "I was sworn to secrecy. And Ann's boyfriends usually don't last long."

"Oh," was all he said.

"About the mine." She licked her cracked lips. "I want to stay home and write."

"What did you say?"

His gaze made her more uncomfortable than the talk about Marty and Ann's secret.

"I need time to write the article."

"So, you want to stay home?" He grinned, turning it into a fake yawn.

"Yes."

"Sure. I'll be able to make it to the mine offices. I'm an expert with this walking stick." He grabbed the bed frame and twirled the stick in the air.

"Thanks, Geoff." She pulled back his bed cover.

"Just make sure you say some nice things about me, especially since my face will be plastered above the article." He sat on the bed. "Otherwise, I'll be forced to type a rebuttal."

~*~

The next morning, Geoff reclined on the couch, eyes closed, hands resting on his stomach.

"Don't worry about breakfast," he said when she had finally made it downstairs. I found the extra rolls and pie."

"Surprised you didn't top it off with a ginger snap."

His eyes opened. "You know me too well."

"You didn't." She tied on her chicken-coop apron. "You'll be on that couch for a while."

"It'll give me time to reminisce about the party.

We organized a topnotch affair."

"We?" She gave him a strict schoolteacher stare.

"I ordered the wine. Your mother liked it."

"My mother enjoyed herself. No one should suffer on a perfect day."

"Almost perfect."

"What do you mean almost? Your brother can hardly wait to come back."

Geoff pulled himself into a sitting position. "Marty. The audacity of that...man inviting you to my mine. I'm the owner, and you're my caregiver." Anger simmered in his words.

She thought Geoff had forgotten about the incident in the kitchen yesterday. She hurried to check on the hens.

A bow-topped box on the dining table caught her eye.

She read the tag. It said, "For Jo" in Geoff's handwriting.

"What's this?" She held up the box.

Geoff sat straighter on the couch.

"It's not my birthday. I thought we decided not to give gifts."

"You never agreed to that." Now he sounded like the teacher. "You insisted on homemade gifts."

She balanced the lightweight rectangular box in her hand. "This doesn't look or feel like a homemade gift."

"I assure you it's as homemade as I can get. Besides, I was too ill to celebrate your eighteenth birthday. After all the work you put into hosting the party, I owe you a gift."

Off came the box top. A navy blue hinged case lay inside. She recognized the jeweler's name. Shooting him an awed glance, she opened the case. Her mouth gaped. An exquisite gold locket—square with a capital "J" engraved on its front, lay in the box. "This is definitely not homemade."

"The gold is from Kat Wil, and I told my father exactly what I wanted, so I followed your rule as best I could. Now, stop grumbling about the rules and tell me what you think."

The smooth-linked chain slipped through her fingers as she admired the locket. "It's gorgeous. I've never seen such a necklace. The engraving even sparkles."

"Happy belated birthday, Josephine Primrose."

She unclasped the chain and hurried over to where he sat.

"Put it on me." She lifted the hair from her neck.

He clasped the locket.

She pressed the golden square against her skin. "I can't believe it's mine. I've never owned anything this stunning." Her eyes celebrated with his. "Thank you."

"You're welcome. But before you start writing for the day, could I have a real breakfast."

"In a minute. I want to see how it looks in the mirror." She ran upstairs holding the locket in place.

"It's the same. Backward maybe."

"It's beautiful," she called from her room. Did Mr. Chambers's mind wander the same path as Ann's after Geoff ordered the locket? Fortunately, she wouldn't have to face the Chambers for a while. Explanations could wait. Her feet pounded down the steps. She flung her arms around Geoff, gently resting her lips on his cheek. "Thank you, so much."

"Now you can't say you're eighteen and never been kissed." He adjusted his pounced-on position.

"A peck on the cheek doesn't count as a first kiss. Besides, I was the giver not the receiver."

"So, you're waiting for a Gregory kiss?" He grinned. "And not on your arm?"

She looked at the fringe on the rug not knowing how to respond. Not knowing much about kissing.

"If you keep fingering that locket, you're going to rub the corners round," he said.

She stilled her hand and excused herself to start breakfast. If truth be told, and she wasn't telling, she was thinking more about kissing Geoff on the lips than kissing Gregory.

~*~

Josephine rose early Wednesday, March 26, to get a few hours of writing in before Tubby arrived to whisk Geoff off to the mine. Sun filtered through the sheers, but no noise filtered from Geoff's bedroom. She knocked on his door.

"Tubby will be here soon. Looks like you caught a break with the weather. No storms."

"I'm not going to the mine." His voice was much too loud and his tone much too short for this time of morning.

Concern emboldened her. "I'm coming in." She opened the door. He reclined on the bed bare-chested, his wooden legs askew on the rug.

"What's wrong?"

"Some bug bit my stump. It's too swollen to fit into its wooden case."

She examined the red-pimpled leg.

"You need to soak this. The rash is spreading. I should be able to fix you up before Tubby gets here."

"Don't trouble yourself. I'll go another day." His fist pounded the bed.

He tilted his head back against the headboard. His eyes dulled. They reminded her of the first time she had sneaked into his room at the mansion.

"If it's urgent for you to get out to the mine, take the chair." She tried to sound encouraging, but even she knew that wheeling cut-off legs down the dock couldn't compare to proudly strolling the planked ramp.

"I'm not going to Kat Wil in the chair."

She envisioned Geoff as a robust soldier crossing roaring rivers and scaling trenches, determined to crush the enemy and return home whole and handsome. It was a cruel hoax. He had returned the same man but in a changed body.

Her gaze bore down on him. "They know about your loss at the mine. If they can't handle seeing your cropped body in a wheelchair, then too bad for them." Pride and a touch of anger roared inside of her. "Now, wash up while I warm some saltwater. I'll dress while you soak the bite, and then we'll see to your wardrobe." She wedged the wheelchair next to the bed.

"You're not coming." He shifted toward the chair. "I don't want you frightened by Edgar Young."

"Oh, I'm coming. With the way you screamed at that man, he won't come near me. And I don't plan on leaving your side. If anyone so much as raises an eyebrow at your legs, I'll unleash a string of words fit only for a Yukon saloon."

"Don't you go accosting any more of my miners with that prickly tongue of yours."

Her face pinked as she remembered her outburst.

Geoff wheeled into the bathroom. His muffled

laughter reverberated through the wall.

At least someone found her rebuttal of those awful accusations funny.

She hurried to get ready, and a few hours later, Tubby was docking the *Maiden* at Kat Wil Mine. She and Geoff disembarked right on schedule. Marty and Mr. Collins greeted them at the end of the platform. Chiseled mountain cliffs loomed in the background dwarfing the welcoming party. Marty's cordial greeting had vanished, leaving his welcome businesslike and aloof.

Wearing sensible shoes with her calf-length skirt and long-sleeved jacket, she hoped to avoid a repeat of her blistered toes. She sat in the office while Geoff pored over accounting statements and payroll ledgers. In the afternoon, Geoff, Marty, and Mr. Collins left the office. Their raised voices echoed off the hollowed earth of the mine.

Heels *clickety-clacked* on the walkway. The noise grew louder, coming closer to the office. Josephine's attention piqued. Women didn't work at the mine. Especially not in heels.

The office door flung open. A petite, curly-haired woman stormed into Marty's headquarters. Her onyx-eyed stare surveyed each desk, and then her gaze scrolled up and down Josephine's suit as if seeking an imperfection.

"Marty around?" The woman sauntered to the cupboard where Marty stored his liquor.

"He stepped out." Josephine tried not to stare at the wavy black and white-striped stockings covering the woman's calves. They looked like slithering snakes peering out from a shorter-than-average skirt. A slip of black lace hung below the hem of her dress. The woman appeared to want to entice more than snakes.

"Want a drink?" the woman asked as if she had a right to offer Marty's whiskey.

"No, thank you. I don't drink." Josephine listened for the men's voices, but all she heard was the squawk of a crane.

Clack, clickety-clack, clack. The woman's cream-strapped heels hammered the floor. A waft of bourbon and smoke and peppermint made Josephine breathe through her mouth. The woman sat awfully close to Josephine.

"How old are you?" The woman's gaze settled on the hint of cleavage below Josephine's locket.

"Eighteen and a half...almost." Josephine softened her voice, trying to sound polite.

The woman glanced at Josephine's hands. Was she looking for a wedding ring? Josephine noticed a lack of a band on the woman's ring finger.

"Could I make some money with you?" The insult purred from the woman's glossed lips. "I haven't seen you in town. Do you live in Douglas?"

Was the woman insinuating what Josephine thought she was insinuating? Josephine thrust her shoulders back in disgust. She knew what type of woman worked at the mine. "I take care of Mr. Chambers. We live up island."

"I see," the woman said, "it's a private arrangement." She seemed happy to clothe Josephine in the same soiled sheets as herself.

Josephine's cheeks flushed. "I assure you, ma'am. It's not like that."

"A man and a woman alone in a lodge?" Her bushy eyebrows rose slightly. "Surely?" The stranger cackled and tapped Josephine's shoulder as if they had shared a joke.

Josephine stiffened.

Footsteps interrupted their conversation.

Mr. Collins held the door open as Geoff wheeled into the room. Marty stilled when he saw the garish woman waiting in his office. A touch of scarlet covered his cheekbones.

"Martin," the woman drawled. "I've come to collect for some of the young ones who believe in IOUs. Can't start the weekend in the red."

"Uh, Wanda. We were—"

"Leaving," Geoff broke in. "Looks like you have some other business to attend to, Marty."

Geoff wheeled to the coat rack. "I have what I came for. Ready to go, Jo?"

Josephine rose to help Geoff gather his things.

Wanda grasped her arm. "I understand now, dear." The woman motioned ever so slightly to the vacant space below Geoff's thighs. Her nose wrinkled as if she smelled a stench.

Acid burned in Josephine's stomach. How dare this woman judge Geoff? Did she think him unworthy to share her squeaky bed?

"No, you don't understand, Madam." Josephine pulled free from the harlot's clutches. She draped her arm over Geoff's shoulder and slid her hand down the front of his coat. "I'm ready to go home now." She patted Geoff's chest and ignored any glances from Marty Hill.

Geoff looked at the woman and then at her and then at Marty. "Wheel away." He rubbed his jaw to conceal a grin.

When they were a good distance down the dock, Geoff asked, "What the heck went on back there? Did that woman say something inappropriate to you?"

Josephine laughed at his curious outburst. "There was a misunderstanding."

"Hers or yours?"

"Definitely hers."

"Did you stand up for my honor?" Geoff shifted in his chair so he could see her face. "Like one of those gallant men in your magazine?"

"Not exactly." She swallowed twice trying to moisten her throat. Her cheeks plumped with embarrassment as she pushed him toward the *Maiden*.

"Aren't you worried about your reputation?"

She scanned the dock to see if anyone was watching their departure. No one was.

"I don't think that woman is too concerned about reputations," she said.

"What if Ann hears about this?"

"She won't. Then Marty would have to explain why a brothel madam calls him Martin."

Geoff shook his head and smirked. He reached up and took her left hand.

"*Merci,* Josephine." Soft kisses grazed her gloved knuckles.

Foreign phrases flowed from his mouth. Her pulse surged with every kiss to her hand.

She decided French was the most beautiful, most provocative, most intriguing language she had ever heard. And when Geoff spoke it, it was magnificent. Even when he spoke it at a dingy mine.

26

Weeks of writing, typing, and worrying had left Josephine feeling like a pinned-up pattern. She took two aspirin to combat a two-day headache. April was ending. The month had flown by, a blur of typewriter keys, wedding dress patterns, and whirlwind rummy sessions.

Geoff had retired early to review invoices, so she sprawled on the paisley rug in front of the Victrola. With her article finished and in the post, and Ann's wedding dress nearly completed, she laid flat on her back, eyes on the ceiling, listening to Irving Kaufman croon about love and ladies. What would it be like to have a beau and sit on his sturdy knee or recline together in a Morris chair? When the visual images caused her heartbeat to quicken and her stomach to flutter, she remembered her mother's warning about keeping thoughts pure. But when the singer's enticing voice summoned her back into the world of relationships, she went willingly.

"What are you listening to?"

She sprang into a sitting position, her chest rising and falling with the notes of the horn section. "*I Love the Ladies*."

Geoff chuckled. "I didn't think my father would

bring that song." He carefully tottered to the Victrola and returned the needle to the beginning of the record.

"Why? Have you been swimmin' with the women?" She startled herself with her boldness and blamed it on Mr. Kaufman.

"Not anymore." He perched in a chair with his wooden legs straight out in front like ski tracks and listened to Irving Kaufman sing about his infatuation. The Victrola crackled and hissed. After a few choruses, Geoff pushed to a stand. "That's enough of that." He shuffled to the corner and removed the record.

She held out the album cover. "You're not going to break it?"

"Of course not." He looked shocked that she would suggest such a thing. "It's not a song for mixed company. There has to be something better in our repertoire." He thumbed through the records and put on a kick-up-your-heels tune.

Ragtime paraded through her temples. "This should be played in the morning. I need music to help me sleep. My shoulders are tight from sewing and beading."

Geoff waved his hands in the air as if conducting a band. "I can relate to sore shoulders."

Her heart skipped. "Did you put our picture in the envelope before you gave it to Tubby? The editorial office requested a photograph."

"Don't worry. Our happy faces are in the envelope with your article. Attention and fame will be yours once May's issue hits the newsstand."

"You think so?" She beamed with the anticipation of seeing her article and story in homes across America. She gazed at the man who critiqued her work, pushed her to write, and pushed her to tell his story. With Geoff's hair cut short, his face clean shaven, and a dimpled smile, she would have done anything he asked of her, within reason. She'd even let him steal kisses and sing about it.

The music stopped.

She replaced the empty static with a ballad of sunshine and roses. Optimistically, she turned to him and asked, "Will you teach me to dance for Ann's wedding? I have until July."

"Dance? I haven't danced since Belleau Wood. The explosion ended my dancing days."

"Just a few steps? An easy foxtrot? I don't want to be a wedding wallflower while everyone else is enjoying themselves."

"Absolutely not. I have no feeling at the end of these pegs. I'm liable to flatten your arches with one misplaced foot. I won't be responsible for crushing your toes." He eased onto the couch.

"I'll be careful. I'll watch both our steps."

"Jo, there are some things I cannot do."

"Try please, for me?" She pulled on his arm hoping he'd stand, but his body did not budge. "Come on. I won't get hurt," she pleaded.

His face stayed serious like when he was determined to win at rummy.

Her mind spun, thinking of ways to get him to stand. A threat.

"I'll sit on your thigh if you don't get up."

His eyes grew wide. "You most certainly will not."

She strolled over to where he sat, fanning her skirt, wrapping it tight to her body as if she was one of those lovely ladies on the record.

He stood and caught her arm. "Don't play like this, or I'll smash that record for sure. Do you hear me?"

All of Douglas Island could hear him. She nodded and tried to swallow, but a lump lodged in her throat. Guilt tainted her silliness. She was too ashamed to look at his face.

He released his hold.

Tapped the table.

And sighed.

"Go get your shoes."

"You'll teach me?" Her voice rose in disbelief.

"You have to have something harmless to do with Marty's friends. You can't be going around teasing men by sitting on their laps."

She bit her lip. She didn't want to be like the woman at the mine flaunting an indecent lifestyle.

"I'm sorry, Geoff. I shouldn't have said what I did."

Lifting her chin so their eyes met, he said, "Go get your mine walking shoes. The pair with the shiny buckles." His dimples reappeared. "I'd also like to see Ann's wedding dress. You've spent a lot of time on it, and well, I'd like to see what you've designed. After all, she is marrying my manager."

"And when everyone sees Ann in my dress, they'll think her too exquisite for that sly codger, Marty Hill."

"Codger?" Geoff laughed as if he was glad someone agreed with his assessment of Marty. "Let me see this transforming creation of yours, Miss Nimetz."

She sauntered toward the stairs.

"Put on Robert Lewis or Irving Kaufman," she said. "No opera."

The up-tempo tune halted.

"Oh, and don't just bring down the dress," he called. "Wear it."

"Wear it!" she repeated, hanging over the railing. "That's bad luck."

"No, it's not. You have to try it on to see if it's made properly."

"Made properly? It's perfect."

"Marty's looking more dapper as we speak." He fanned himself with the record cover.

"Don't say that. Besides, it's a bit too long for me."

"What isn't?"

She crossed her arms.

"Look, I'm teaching you how to dance with no opera records, and I'll even play with Riley in the morning. That's a good deal."

"Oh, all right," she said, "but you have to feed Riley, too. And the hens."

"Deal. But don't slip coming down in that wedding dress, or I'll have some explaining to do about my intentions."

Robert Lewis's crooning drowned out his laughter.

Ann's gown glided easily over Josephine's hips. Ann was fuller through the waist, but not in the chest. Josephine held her breath and zipped up the dress. She admired herself in the mirror. On her wedding day, she would definitely wear something less formal and with less beading. Carefully, she stepped down the staircase.

"My goodness. Are there any beads left in the Yukon Territory? You look like an archangel floating down those steps." His eyes marveled at the sparkling design. "You've outdone yourself."

"So, you think Ann will like it?" She twirled and soaked up his attention.

"Yes. Marty better be on his best behavior, or there will be a line of men ready to take his place at the altar." Geoff took her hand. "Miss Nimetz, designer, seamstress, and writer extraordinaire, may I have this dance?"

"Only if you promise not to step on my gown."

She stood on her tiptoes and placed her right hand on his shoulder. He laced her left hand with his right. His left hand rested on her upper back. When she swung her head, her hair caught on his arm.

"Stand up straight." He grew even taller than six feet as he puffed out his chest. "And don't lean into me. The last thing you, or I, need is a broken back."

"How's this?" She stretched to her full height.

"At least I can see the top of your forehead." He shifted awkwardly. "Roll your shoulders back."

She perfected her posture. "Why?"

"There's supposed to be space between us."

"Oh," was all she said.

"Yeah, well, let's begin." He cleared his throat. A pink hue shaded his cheeks. "I will take two slow steps forward. The slower the better. At least 'til we see how this goes. If I start forward with my left foot, you start backward with your...?"

"Right," she said, her gaze intent on their feet.

"After two slow steps, we're supposed to do a quick step to the side, but since I'm half lumber, diagonal steps will have to suffice."

"If you go left side diagonal, then I'm going right?"

"Exactly. Ready to try it with no injuries?"

When she perused her feet, her hair draped over his arm.

"I should put my hair in a bun. It's in your way."

"It's fine. I like how long it's gotten. My mother had long hair. Sometimes when I was a boy and couldn't sleep, she'd set me on the rug near her dressing area, and I'd watch her brush her cascading light-brown hair. 'Fifty strokes to entice the men folk' she used to say. I never knew if she got to fifty strokes. My eyelids sealed shut by forty."

She waited as he took hold again, being careful not to apply any backward pressure to his body. His steps—calculated at first—couldn't keep rhythm to the beat of the music. She mirrored his every move, never running ahead or taking charge of the dance.

By the third record, they had learned to keep better time. Perspiration glistened on Geoff's temples. He mastered every step. His breaths winded the side of her face.

"You smell different," he said, "like a flower garden."

She laughed as he sniffed her neck, tickling her skin with his nose. "It's Cashmere Bouquet. A gift from Tubby for being the first person he knows to be featured in a magazine. I think he saw the ad on the back of the *Companion*."

"Well, he didn't see it in any sailor's rag. And he didn't get me anything. The article is about me."

She giggled at his envy. "You didn't expect anything, did you? Toiletries are not a manly gift."

"I could use some right now."

"You smell fine. One more dance?" Her gown shimmered under the light.

"You mean shuffle, don't you?" he said, critiquing his own style.

"You're a superb teacher and dancer. A bit stiff, but I don't know any different." She laughed at the pout in his lips. "You must save me a dance at the wedding."

"You won't have any trouble getting a dance with me. I, on the other hand, will probably have to wait in line all night."

"I doubt that."

His hand cupped her shoulder. "But no one can cut in tonight."

As the Victrola played on, the space between their bodies evaporated. She felt his chest rise and fall with every breath. Her skin tingled under the touch of his body, sparking a burning in the depths of her belly. She longed to push into him. Instead, she focused on their feet, not wanting the night to end with injury.

The music stopped.

He kept her in hold.

Their upper bodies swayed while his feet remained firmly planted on the floor.

"I don't know what it is about long hair that mesmerizes me, but I can hardly keep my eyes open." He pulled away from her and steadied himself.

"Was I leaning?" she asked.

"Since the last song. I'm still standing." He slid his hand down her arm. "Your next partner should be easier to follow. He may actually be able to step backward."

"Thanks for the dance lesson." She couldn't help but smile. They had actually danced somewhat. With no collisions. She gazed into his wide-awake eyes. Was he waiting for a thank you? Rising on tiptoe, she kissed him. Softly, yet full on the lips.

She pulled away; ready to run up the stairs.

He grasped her hand and held her in position.

"Don't steal a kiss from me and run away." His gaze intensified as if he wanted to teach her more than the foxtrot. "Give your partner a chance to kiss you back."

She blushed. "Do you want to kiss me back?"

He did not pull away. Instead, he stroked her neck and then cupped the back of her head. His lips came closer. His breath tickled her mouth. She stilled like a statue as his lips brushed against hers. They were soft and tender and then gone.

Bouncing, she kissed him. With a longer kiss. A wonderful kiss. A lingering kiss.

He parted their bodies. "Dance lessons are over." He inhaled deep.

"What if I don't want them to be over?"

"Jo, my body is bursting with life. I feel like going over the top, and I'm not talking about a trench. If you don't dash up those stairs, I'll scarcely make it to my room to pull off these legs."

"I'll help you remove them."

Geoff burst out with a laugh. "That won't help me."

"But the Victrola?"

His hands caught her waist. "I'll see to the records." He pushed her toward the stairs. "I might have to censor a few."

Her dress rustled as she lifted it so she wouldn't trip on the stair. She didn't want their dance partnership to end. "Good night, partner."

Grinning, he said, "I'm sure it will be."

Ascending the stairs, she inspected where the hem puddled on each step. Her body throbbed with a pleasurable warmth, but she would not allow one misplaced heel to ruin Ann's dress. It only took a moment to strip out of Ann's gown and collapse onto the bed. She pressed her stomach against the firm mattress as she tried to smother the smoldering embers sparking below her belly button. Lust pinned her to the bed. Her conscience knew which bed she desired to be in. Geoff's bed. Ann's words mocked her, "bedding a cripple?" She had to tame these wayward thoughts.

She rolled on her back, clutching a pillow to her chest. Thunder shook her senses. A storm drifted closer to the lodge. Was it God's wrath judging her impure thoughts? Lightning lit up the bedroom. She hugged the pillow tighter.

Nesting into the covers, she tried to clear her mind and ignore the brilliant flashes of light banishing the darkness. She cocooned into the warmth of the sheets.

Movement by her bed startled her. She knew it was Geoff by the drag of his legs.

Thunder raged.

He slid closer.

"Are you scared, Jo?"

She shook her head. Her voice had vanished.

He perched on the side of the bed. "I can protect you." His comforting touch awakened her skin.

Her lips tingled from his firm kiss.

She wanted him to keep her warm and safe through the night. Through this storm.

Her pillow fell to the ground. Cool night air chilled her legs and feet. She woke with a start. Plunging forward, her hand covered her mouth. Her eyes searched the room. She was alone. All alone. She would have sworn he had been there.

How could she have such a bawdy dream? She cared for Geoff, but he wasn't her beau or sweetheart. How could she face him in the morning after summoning him into her fantasy?

Thunder trailed off over the mountains. She wrapped herself in bed sheets. A whirlwind of emotions swirled inside her body.

Only six more weeks.

What would it be like when she and Geoff returned to Juneau? Would he avoid her? Would he acknowledge her if they met on the street? Would he introduce her to the likes of Brice Todd? Would he greet her, tip his hat, and walk away? He didn't need her anymore. Then why, oh why, did she feel she needed him? And not just in her dreams.

27

The next morning, Josephine tiptoed down the stairs. Geoff's bedroom doors were closed. She didn't want to wake him. A plume of feathers still tickled her chest from their kiss the night before.

A vase of fern fronds and flower buds decorated the kitchen counter.

"'Bout time you got up." Geoff's voice was as cheerful as the flora.

She turned. Geoff stood in the corner near the door.

His eyes widened with his grin. "I heard you on the stairs."

"I was trying not to wake you."

"I've been up for hours. Riley and I've been outside surveying the property. That dog took me to places I never knew existed."

"So, I have you to thank for the muddy paw prints on the floor."

"And the bouquet."

He strolled toward her as if to take up a dance hold.

A wave of want built in the pit of her stomach and swelled into her ribs. She thought she might melt right there on the kitchen floor.

His head dipped low. His Adam's apple bobbed. "I got caught up in the music last night. I didn't mean to scare you with my kiss"

Her throat parched. "You didn't scare me. It was a thank you for the dance." She brushed by him and moved toward the sink. "I haven't started the bread for today."

"Is that what you're worried about?" He rubbed his stubbly beard.

She nodded.

He angled himself toward the living room. "I'll let you get to work then. You know what they say. If you want to marry a man and share his pillow, you have to cook up something delicious for his stomach."

Her heart was bouncing all over her chest. He said marry. Surely, he didn't mean *them*? What did Geoff envision with her now that their time together was almost over? Did he see a future as husband and wife or envision a sinful night in his bed? He wouldn't need her services when they returned to Juneau. He was capable of handling most of his care on his own. The Chambers Estate had plenty of servants who could assist him now that he was healthy.

She opened the kitchen door.

Riley sat on the porch and watched her as if he was expecting her to throw him some tidbits.

The dew-scented air made her forget about breakfast and Geoff and their dance. It was too nice a morning to stay indoors. Taking a quick break from thoughts and feelings, she followed Riley to nowhere.

~*~

"You seem antsy." Geoff viewed her over the four

cards he held in his rummy hand.

It had been two weeks since their kiss and almost that long since May's issue of *Woman's Home Companion* had been released. Their issue.

"Just trying to keep my winning streak alive." She laid the nine of clubs down on his trio of nines and placed her last card—the ace of spades—on his two, three, four run. Empty handed, she said, "Gin."

His cards flew across the table. "You deal. This time maybe my luck will change."

She shuffled and dealt the cards. She even turned her back when he sorted his hand. No one was going to accuse her of cheating. The squeal of gulls interrupted her concentration.

"Are you expecting Tubby today?" She pulled back the window sheers. Excitement streaked through her veins. The *Maiden* was docked in the inlet. Tubby should have a copy of her article with him. "Tubby's here."

Geoff balanced on his walking stick.

She sorted cards and cleaned off the coffee table.

"Yep, it's Tubby." Geoff watched the ship from the window. "Probably made the trip especially for you."

Josephine opened the front door.

"Who are those men with him? I've never seen the crew wearing sack suits and soft-crowned hats."

Geoff came up behind her. "I can't believe it." His voice sounded as cheery as Christmas morning. "Brice is here. And it looks like Doc Miller." He shuffled quickly toward the dock. She followed at a distance not wanting to interfere with Geoff's greeting of his guests.

Geoff and Brice embraced. They slapped each other's shoulders and gave each other what looked like a military inspection. Doc Miller received a handshake from his former patient.

"Josephine." Dr. Miller held out his hand. "You're the image of your mother. I saw Sophia at the beginning of the week. Her arthritis is much improved."

"I noticed when she visited. In no time, she'll be taking dress orders for me."

"Jo...sephine, you remember Mr. Todd." Geoff indicated his boyhood friend. "Brice, Miss Josephine Nimetz."

"We've met." Brice shook her hand, limp wristed. He glanced at the lodge appearing more interested in the house than his hostess.

Tubby waved May's issue of *Woman's Home Companion* above his cap.

"Bet you've been waiting for this. I've got letters from some of the ladies in town. You're the talk of Juneau. Wish I could stick around and take a peek at their praises, but I'm dropping Dr. Miller off at Kat Wil before returning for Mr. Todd."

Josephine flipped through the pages to catch a glimpse of her picture. "It's nothing serious at the mine, is it? I was hoping you could stay for lunch?"

"Maybe another time," the doctor replied. "There's a few cases of pneumonia."

Geoff and Brice abandoned the dock and chatted all the way to the lodge. After giving her regards to Tubby, she hurried after them. She jumped a few rocks and thought she might soar right into the sky.

Tossing the bundle of letters on the first stair, she opened the magazine and displayed the article to Geoff.

"Look," she said between breaths, "our picture is right up top."

Geoff showed the photograph to Brice while Josephine took their guest's hat and coat.

Brice peered at the page. "Except for that stick, no one would guess you're injured."

"They haven't seen me move." Geoff flailed his arms as if he was about to tilt over.

"Careful," Josephine cautioned.

Geoff's expression sobered.

"Lucky for you, Josephine, you serve such a courageous man. Not many people would want to share their war demons with the world." Brice sat in her chair, making himself at home. "Without Geoff, you wouldn't have had a story to sell."

She stiffened. "I wrote another story for the magazine. The editor inquired about my position and asked me to write an article about Geoff's recovery."

"Did they?" Brice didn't sound convinced.

"The *Companion* makes plenty of money selling serials to ladies." Geoff handed her the magazine. "Josephine can't get her fill fast enough. And real-life drama adds to the fiction."

"Fortunately, Margaret is drawn to non-fiction like me," Brice said. "She's quite the sensible woman."

"Margaret?" Josephine glanced up from skimming the article.

"Brice's girlfriend." Geoff furrowed his brow at her interruption before turning his attention back to Brice.

"Soon to be fiancé," Brice added. "I plan on heading to New York the first part of July to convince her to return to Juneau with me."

"New York or Juneau? Hmmm. Too bad you're not a bigger draw," Geoff chided.

The men laughed.

Brice leaned forward. "You should come along. Captain Barrie mentioned you were planning on returning home the beginning of June. Change of scenery would do you good." Brice surveyed the inside of the lodge. He inspected the bear's head above the mantel.

Geoff adjusted the position of his right leg. "Certainly sounds like fun. I don't know though. It's not easy traveling in my condition."

"Margaret has a friend who's a nurse. I'm sure she's run into men in your state of health before."

Fire blazed in Josephine's belly. She gripped the back of a dining room chair and almost hurled it at know-it-all Brice. Geoff didn't need a big city, book-learned nurse. She cared for Geoff's cracked and tormented body with almost no training. How could Brice waltz into her home and whisk Geoff away to New York?

Josephine excused herself to prepare soup for lunch. Soon, warm bread, soft butter, and honey-drizzled fruit cups adorned the table.

"Who's joining us for lunch?" Brice asked, indicating the three place settings.

She tilted her head and waited for Geoff to answer.

Geoff met her dare-you gaze. He shrugged ever so slightly.

"Uh, it's easier for Josephine to serve this way before she goes upstairs to her room." His eyes pleaded with her to accept his lie.

Serve? Was that all she was to Geoff? A young Mrs. Prescott? Her ears buzzed. Her muscles tensed. *Be nice.* She didn't want to embarrass Geoff or give Brice any reason to think that she or her family was even more inferior than he already thought.

"I'm sure you two have plenty to talk about that would be of no interest to me." She kept her tone polite and cheerful. "I have plenty of letters to read."

She bit her lip and forced a smile as she served chicken soup. Balancing a tray in one hand, she planted a brass bell in front of Geoff. "You can summon me when you're ready for dessert, Mr. Chambers."

"Beats a broom handle on the ceiling," Brice chuckled. "Remember? Mrs. Prescott nearly quit after supervising us for the weekend."

Reminiscent joking followed her upstairs. Anger knotted her jaw muscles. Banished to her room, she chewed every piece of chicken and vegetable in her soup to a pulp. How could Geoff send her to her room after kissing her with such passion? Perhaps Ann was right; Geoff only wanted to coax her into his bed before time ran out.

Remaining upstairs would have been unbearable except for the fact that she got to read her article over and over and over. Bold letters declared Josephine Nimetz had authored this piece. She admired her photograph. Hues of gray favored her complexion.

When curiosity got the best of her, she pressed her ear to the floorboards hoping to eavesdrop on Geoff and Brice. Their muffled words hardly carried past the fourth stair. Why had Mr. Gilbertsen built such a solid lodge?

Ring-a-ling.

A summons from Geoff.

She lingered on every stair as if she was saying good-bye to it.

"I hear congratulations are in order," Brice said as

she entered the dining room. "You and Geoff will practically be related when your sister marries Marty Hill."

"Thank you." Had the meal helped Brice find his civil side? "I am happy for Ann."

"Mr. Hill will provide a nice living for your sister. They'll be no need for you to keep Geoff out here at the lodge." Brice elbowed Geoff as if they shared a secret.

Where was the potted plant she hid behind on her first encounter with Brice Todd? She'd like to throw it in his face. Dirt and all.

"I assure you, Brice," she made his name hiss. "Geoff is free to leave the lodge at any time. In fact, I've encouraged it."

"Tea please." Geoff cleared his throat. "Do we have any of your delicious ginger snaps?"

If he was trying to appease her by accentuating de-li-cious, it worked. A little.

"We have a few. I wasn't expecting company." She removed the dirty china from the table and set tea cups in front of the men.

She couldn't believe she had once found Brice attractive. His thinning blond hair, coiffed to perfection, couldn't hide his bald spot. His nose, a bit more prominent than she remembered, diminished the intensity of his blue eyes. Geoff's aquamarine eyes shone like sun on water.

"It must have been lonely for you," Brice said, his gaze solely on Geoff. "It's too bad you couldn't have returned to Juneau sooner. Got caught up in all that story business, did you?"

"Not ex—"

"Geoff encouraged me to write about his injuries." She set the tea service on the table. "We've been busy, too. Going to the mine. Entertaining family. I do earn my keep."

Brice scoffed as if he had a piece of chicken caught in his throat. "Don't you mean you're kept to earn."

"You're mistaken about our arrangement." She ignored etiquette and poured Geoff a cup of tea before their guest. She fought to keep her hands from shaking. She would not give Brice the satisfaction of knowing he unnerved her.

She reached to pour Brice some tea, having half a mind to pour it on his head.

Brice lifted the saucer closer to the pot.

Scalding liquid splattered on Brice's hand.

Brice flinched. He cradled his hand in his lap. "Stupid girl."

She jumped backward as if she had been burned. Brice's curses rang in her ears. "I'm sorry."

Geoff struggled to stand.

"Let me wrap it for you." She raced to get a cold cloth.

Returning, she reached to cover the burn. Brice jerked. His forearm struck her in the stomach.

She stumbled backward and dropped to the floor.

"Don't touch me," Brice shouted.

"Jo," Geoff gasped. "Are you—?"

She didn't let Geoff finish.

"See to your friend," she said as a bruising ache radiated through her tailbone. "He doesn't want to be handled by the hired help."

She sprinted through the kitchen and out the back door. Humiliation stung her eyes. She raced toward the water, cutting through the Douglas firs, letting the woods hide her from Brice and Geoff. She didn't want to face either of them. The spill was an accident. Brice's hand would heal, and another apology would drain any self-esteem she had left. She kept running, following the curve of the inlet. Her lungs burned hot from her hurried pace.

Resting against the crumbling bark of a tree, she looked up at layered pine branches stacked to the heavens. She felt small and insignificant. Is that what Brice had wanted? If it was, he deserved a prize.

Movement caught her attention.

A twig snapped.

She froze.

A bear moved through the underbrush.

Keep on going.

The bear lumbered away. Brawny muscles quaked beneath its shiny black fur.

She released her breath.

Branches rustled. Growls ricocheted through the woods. Riley snapped playfully at the paws of a bear cub. The cub cried in protest.

"Riley," she called, hoping to interrupt his chase.

Her dog broke his pursuit. He bounded toward her. Too late.

The mother bear began to charge. Straight for Riley. Straight for her.

She turned and sprinted toward the lodge. Her legs spun faster and faster. She needed a rifle to save herself and to save her dog.

Riley followed her. He veered right. She glanced to see where he was going. His tail whipped in circles as he cut back and resumed his chase of the cub. The mother bear halted her charge to protect her baby.

Thank heavens.

Crack.

Pain radiated through her face and spread into her

skull. She was falling, floating horizontally in the air. Her right hand shot out to keep her head from crashing into the ground. Dirt moistened her palm. Her wrist bent. Ouch! More pain radiated up her arm as she slammed into the ground.

The taste of antique silver seeped into her mouth. She fingered her cheek. Blood.

She tried to rise. The landscape spun. Her stomach surged. She clamped her eyes shut to relieve the nausea.

Lying on her back, she heard a rapid panting coming her direction. She prayed it was Riley. *Please be my dog.*

A spongy tongue licked her cheek. Her fear calmed. She grabbed Riley's fur and tried to halt his licking. She wanted to go home and take him with her, but her head would not budge from the ground.

"Home," she mumbled, "go home."

She thought she heard a faint voice. Was it real? Or was it the pounding in her forehead? Was that her name?

Her temples pulsed, mocking her stupidity.

Riley's ears perked up. He ran.

Her pet left her alone. Alone and injured in the forest's shadows.

She rolled onto her side. Her head throbbed something fierce.

Not again. She began to cry. Gabled roofs and wrap around porches weren't visible through the thick canopy of pines. This wasn't Juneau. No mansion waited for her in these woods.

28

She struggled to rise with one arm. Tree branches see-sawed around her.

"Geoff," she shouted. The taste of bile and herbed chicken filled her mouth. She had to get back to the lodge.

"Cap'n, over here," someone yelled.

"Thank You, Lord."

Tubby crouched over her. "Good heavens. You're a mess." Light from his lantern caused her eyelids to flicker. "We've got to clean up that pretty face of yours."

"My wrist. It hurts. I can't move anything below my elbow."

Tubby eased her arm onto her stomach. "Don't want that dangling when we move you."

She shuddered when he picked her up. Her head ached. Her belly ached. Her wrist ached.

Tears streamed from her eyes. She was in a mess. She was a mess. Why did she have to run from the lodge? Why didn't she retreat to her room and wait for Brice to leave? How was she going to take care of Geoff now that she couldn't move her arm?

"Now, now. Don't cry. Dr. Miller's at the mine.

I'm going to take you to him. Don't worry about a thing little lady."

"Geoff," she mumbled against Tubby's warm coat. "Someone needs to stay with him."

"Brice is at the lodge. Those two can figure it out."

Tubby moved through the trees, swaying and dipping. She clamped her mouth shut to keep from vomiting. The vision of the *Maiden* bobbing on the water unsettled her stomach. The pounding of Tubby's boots on the dock echoed in her skull. She breathed in the cool sea air and tried not to panic.

The staccato beat of Geoff's walking stick rang out over the water.

"Jo, I'm going with you."

"I don't have time to look after you Chambers." Tubby's voice was too loud for her tender head. The captain placed her in another sailor's arms. The smell of gasoline and smoke assaulted her nostrils.

"I want to be with her," Geoff continued.

"Should have thought of that before you sent her fleeing into the woods. I can't be worrying about you falling. I've got to get Jo to Kat Wil."

She wanted to reassure Geoff she'd be fine, but she didn't have the strength to argue. Her body wanted to sleep, and she was too tired to fight the slumber.

"You'll come back." Geoff's voice was fading. "Tomorrow?"

"Enjoy the lodge tonight, boys," Tubby yelled.

Those were the last booming words she heard.

~*~

The lights of the mine were like a thousand Christmas candles illuminating the mountainside. She squinted at their brightness. The same fuel-scented clothes jostled against her side as she was carried off the *Maiden*.

"Is that blood?" Marty asked, surprise in his voice. "What happened?"

"I took a spill in the woods," she answered. "I need to wash my face. It won't look so bad in the morning."

"What were you doing out in the woods? And what in blazes am I going to tell Ann?" Marty opened the door to the infirmary. The pungent smell of isopropyl alcohol rallied her senses. "She'll want to come out to the mine."

"Don't tell Ann anything. Please, Marty."

Her escort slowed his steps.

"Wait until I see the doctor."

"And then?"

"I don't know. But I don't want to upset Ann or my mother. Their focus should be on the wedding."

"We'll see." Marty's voice softened at the mention of his upcoming nuptials.

The crewman placed her on a flimsy plastic mattress. When the hint of weight settled upon her arm, she winced.

Five beds lined her side of the long sterile room. Every bed was empty, except for hers. The other side housed the same number of beds. Blanketed bodies occupied two beds at the other end of the room.

Tubby approached with an armful of pillows and blankets. Doc Miller followed in his wake. She welcomed the extra blankets the captain had confiscated.

"Will she be safe here?" Tubby stared at the forms in the other beds.

"There's an orderly checking on that one." Marty pointed to the farthest bed. "He's bad with pneumonia. He won't be any trouble. Dr. Miller gave him pills to sleep. The other soul's been medicated, too."

Tubby scratched his whiskers. His gaze darted between her and the two men. "I'm not leaving Jo alone. This is precious cargo."

"I'll arrange for some female company for Josephine tonight." Marty patted Tubby's shoulder. "You can return your crew to Juneau. I can't begin to think of how I would explain any mishaps to my future bride."

"I'll be back this way first thing in the morning. Rest up, Jo." Tubby kissed her cheek. He stopped briefly to talk with Dr. Miller.

Marty escorted Tubby out of the infirmary while Dr. Miller lingered at her bedside.

"Well, well, you were the picture of health this morning." Dr. Miller draped a stethoscope over his tweed vest.

"That was before my dog decided to play with a bear cub. I ran into a branch when the mother bear charged me." Her attempt at a smile cracked the dried blood on her cheek.

The silver-haired doctor lifted her bangs and inspected the gash on her forehead.

The pull of her skin made her stomach roll on an imaginary wave.

"Please don't cut my hair." It had taken months to grow out, and she didn't want to be mistaken for a boy again. Once was enough. "I'll tie it back."

"I can work around your hair. Your temple needs a few stitches, but no rest for the weary. The tree gave you a concussion." The doctor turned his attention to her arm. He tried to straighten it.

"Ow, ow, ow." Her left hand squeezed the mattress so hard it thinned to the thickness of a sheet of paper. Rapid breaths chanted from her mouth as the doctor squeezed her wrist. "Is it broken?"

"Afraid so." The doctor wrapped her arm with a cloth bandage. "A sling for now until the swelling goes down. I'd give you something for pain, but that would make keeping you awake nearly impossible."

"You won't mention my accident, will you?" She shimmied her back against the pillows.

Dr. Miller chuckled. He threaded cat gut through a needle. "It's Marty you should be worried about. Don't know if he can hold up under the interrogation of your sister. I wouldn't dare get Juneau's favorite writer in trouble."

The doctor placed a warm, iodine-soaked washcloth on her forehead.

Every muscle in her body seized. Her fingernails embedded into her palm. Was that iodine or rock salt on that rag? She had done a thousand stitches, but not on skin. Her back arched when the needle pin-pricked her forehead. Closing her eyes, she tried not to hyperventilate.

The *clickety-clack* of heels caught her attention. Through a haze of searing pain, she spied the ruby-lipped smirk of the madam at Marty's side. Josephine tensed.

"Wanda, you remember Miss Nimetz?" Marty pulled a chair toward Josephine's bed.

"Ann's baby sister. Of course, I remember." Wanda flared her skirt and lounged in the chair. Fortunately, the striped leggings were gone or hidden by the longer skirt. Josephine didn't think she could look upon those dizzying stockings tonight.

The familiar scent of peppermint and tobacco wafted toward Josephine. No whiskey soured Wanda's breath. At least with Wanda sober and at her side, Josephine wouldn't have to worry about unwanted visitors.

"Wanda's offered to stay with you. Captain's orders," Marty said.

"Absolutely no sleeping, young lady," Dr. Miller warned. "I'll be in tomorrow to see how that wrist's doing."

No sleeping? How would she keep her eyelids open when it felt like an anchor rested on each one? "I'll do my best."

Dr. Miller nodded and strolled in the direction of the men in the far beds.

As soon as Marty and Dr. Miller left the room, Wanda hopped to her feet and inspected Josephine's wrist.

"Not bad," Wanda said, "I've seen worse. One pointing due north even." She lifted Josephine's bangs.

Josephine gasped. She shivered as Wanda's fingers grazed her stitches.

"Won't hardly notice that scar with all your hair." Wanda's hand slid down and stroked Josephine's neck. She fingered Geoff's locket. "Bet they'll be more jewelry waiting for you when you go back to Mr. Chambers."

"I won't be going back to Mr. Chambers." Regret swelled her windpipe. She struggled to swallow. She never dreamed her time with Geoff would end this way. How would she explain the injuries to her mother? Maybe Tubby could collect her possessions from the lodge and steal Riley away on the *Maiden*.

"Don't tell me your arrangement isn't working out?" Wanda stifled a laugh.

Josephine's head sank back into the pillows.

"I can't take care of Mr. Chambers with one arm."

"Don't you fall asleep?" Wanda patted Josephine's cheeks. "I've been paid well to sit here and do nothing all night except keep your eyes open. Easy money." The bed jiggled as Wanda propped her worn-heels on the mattress.

Beige stockings became visible. Good. No bold patterns graced the bedding.

"You're from Juneau?" Wanda's gaze swept over the room.

"Yes, mostly. You?"

"Boise. My papa came up here to strike it rich in the Klondike Rush. I was fourteen when he got gold fever."

"Did he stake a claim?" Josephine hoped the conversation would keep her awake.

Wanda jumped to her feet and paced around the bed opening canisters of gauze and swabs as if they held special gifts. "A few. They never amounted to much. My mother cooked for the men on the trail. She made enough money to support my brother and me. When she took sick, I did the cooking." Wanda grinned. "I made more money than mama."

Watching Wanda parade around the bed made Josephine sleepy. "How'd you get to Douglas Island?"

"Took up with a prospector heading this way. We stayed together for a year and then one morning he boarded a sternwheeler and never came back." Wanda stuffed a few bandages in her dress pocket before sitting down. "Been a businesswoman ever since."

"I'm sorry he left."

"Don't be, darling. Douglas Island's been good to me. I live in a two-story house, I've got money in the bank, and there's plenty of entertainment." Wanda's wistful cackle disturbed a patient at the far end of the room. "And spending the night with a stranger is right up my alley." Wanda scooted her chair closer to the bed.

"I read your article in the *Companion*. Is it all true?"

"About what?" Josephine's heart rate sped. Marty knew what he was doing having Wanda keep her awake. Who else would pry into her private life at the lodge?

"Falling in love with a man with no legs. You do love him, don't you?"

Josephine shifted her throbbing arm into a more comfortable position.

"I never wrote that in the article."

"I saw it when you were here at the mine together. And it's in the picture. You're wide-eyed and smiling like a princess. Why go through all that nonsense if you don't care?"

"Maybe I do."

"That maybe has a bit of a yes in it, doesn't it?" Wanda arched her eyebrows. She plopped down on the bed. Cotton balls rolled out of her pocket. "Don't you find his form distracting?"

"Form?" Josephine remembered the night she had tumbled onto Geoff and discovered his legs were missing. That incident might as well have been a lifetime ago.

"He's not all there. Is he?" Wanda winked seductively.

"Legs? Or…oh." Josephine's cheeks blazed. "I've seen Geoff's legs for so long, I'm able to see past the stumps to the whole man." She met Wanda's curious gaze. "And he is a whole man."

"Geoff?" Wanda giggled.

"Uh, Mr. Chambers."

Wanda shifted back to her chair.

"I'll be interested in reading your story next month. My advice," she added, kicking her heels back up on the bed, "hold out for a big piece of jewelry. Mr. Chambers can afford it."

"He didn't cause my injuries." *I did.*

"Then send the gold my way. With as torn up as you look, you're bound to get something valuable."

Josephine didn't want to think about Geoff or jewelry. The day had started out with sunshine and fern bouquets, but it had ended with injury and broken bones. She worried about Geoff falling at the lodge. Would Brice be any real help?

By nine thirty the next morning, even with Wanda's stories and clacking heels, Josephine struggled to stay awake. A streak of adrenaline brightened her expressions when Marty and Dr. Miller entered the infirmary.

"It's about time you two showed up," Wanda said. "You didn't tell me I'd have to converse all night, Martin. I'm in desperate need of a drink." Wanda tapped Josephine's pillow. "Remember my advice. Heal slow." With a wink, Wanda excused herself. Her pockets bulged with confiscated bandages.

Dr. Miller eased Josephine's arm out of the sling. A burning sensation sizzled in her wrist. She shook as if she was lying atop the Mendenhall Glacier.

"I can give you something for the pain," Dr. Miller said. He removed a syringe from his leather case. A familiar vile graced the doctor's hand.

"I don't need relief. Aspirin is all." She pulled the sheet over her limp arm.

"A little morphine will relax you and help you catch up on your rest." Dr. Miller dabbed alcohol onto a cotton ball.

"No, thank you. I don't like morphine. Mr. Chambers took that drug." She edged away from the doctor and closer to her future brother-in-law. "Please. I promise to be still."

"Settle down young lady." The doctor's voice sharpened. "A shot of morphine will calm your nerves. You can't be wiggling all over while I treat that wrist."

"I won't move. I'll be the best patient."

"Marty, hold her still, will you." Dr. Miller plunged the needle inside the morphine vial.

Marty obeyed. He slipped an arm behind her back and wrapped another across her chest. One arm was uncomfortably high and one arm was uncomfortably low. His hand anchored her hip to the bed.

"Don't fight the doctor," Marty ordered.

"Let go of me."

She wiggled to free herself from Marty's grip. His hold tightened. The waist-high sheet and blanket pinned her limbs to the mattress.

"Please. Don't." Her voice squeaked. "Send me home."

Dr. Miller towered over the bed. "This will only sting for a moment, and then you'll be nice and relaxed."

She felt the cool swipe of alcohol against her skin. "I only need an aspirin." Her muscles knotted. She attempted to rock herself free from Marty's hold, but he was a boulder upon her body. "Don't," she screamed.

The door banged open.

Dr. Miller turned and dropped the syringe.

"Pierce her skin and I'll pierce yours." Geoff's threatening voice took command of the infirmary.

And of her heart.

29

Marty sprang off the bed.

She struggled to catch her breath.

Dr. Miller stepped back into the cabinet, clinking the jars of swabs.

"Mr. Chambers? I didn't expect to see you." Dr. Miller adjusted his stethoscope.

With every step closer, Geoff jabbed his walking stick into the floor.

"Josephine was in a frenzy," Dr. Miller stuttered. "I was calming her down. It's what's best for my patient." He shoved his hands in his coat pockets.

Marty headed toward the infirmary door. "Now that you're here to assist Dr. Miller, I think I'll return to the office."

Geoff stopped Marty's exit with his wooden cane. "If I ever see your arms around Josephine again, I'll need a new balancing stick."

Marty nodded, his gaze never meeting Geoff's glare. "Understood, Mr. Chambers."

Geoff eased onto the bed. Air whooshed from the mattress as he shared her backrest.

"I believe Jo needs an aspirin." Geoff laid a protective arm around her shoulders.

She collapsed into the warmth of Geoff's chest. She thought she smelled a hint of her Cashmere Bouquet on his jacket.

"I'll be fine now." She straightened her elbow allowing Dr. Miller to examine her wrist. "Geoff can hold me still."

"We'll need to splint this arm. I'll check its healing when I remove your stitches next week in Juneau." Dr. Miller rummaged through a cabinet drawer. "I have to check in on your mother."

"She won't be staying in Juneau," Geoff answered. "I'm taking her home to the lodge."

She turned to look at Geoff. A dull ache throbbed in her forehead. She winced.

"It's too much," she said, sinking into Geoff's embrace for support. "I'll be a burden."

"She's correct." Dr. Miller measured a splint against her arm. "There can be no use of this arm for four weeks, and she must rest for the next couple of days."

"I understand your concern, Dr. Miller. But I'm not the man you treated in Juneau. I can take care of myself and Jo. I've had experience with removing stitches." Geoff squeezed her shoulder.

She batted her eyes and tried to not cry. Geoff had removed her stitches. The stitches Ivan had given her. But it was her job to take care of him. He shouldn't have to fuss over her injuries.

Geoff held her arm while the doctor wrapped it. Her veteran's gentle touch and reassuring glances ignited her soul.

"I'll make arrangements to visit you at the lodge then." Dr. Miller packed up his bag. "Get plenty of rest. And no stairs for a few days."

"Understood." Geoff answered in a serious, military voice.

"Thank you," she said, but Dr. Miller had already shifted his attention to the spastic coughing of the man in the last bed.

"Maybe Dr. Miller is right," she whispered. "I can go back to Juneau and work something out with Ann."

"Don't go." Geoff stroked her hair with a wisp of a caress. "I don't want you to leave. I don't want our time together to end this way. I can do this. It's my turn to take care of you."

She uncovered her legs and moved to the edge of the mattress.

"You can't take care of both of us."

He stopped her from leaving the bed. His gaze locked on hers. "I can and I will. I'm going to make this right. I'm ashamed of the way I acted with Brice." He wrapped her good hand in his and lifted it to his face. His breath bathed her fingertips. "Forgive me, Jo. I should have remembered what Brice was like. I should have defended you and told Brice how much you've done for me. Please, come home with me."

"Home?"

"To our home. At the lodge."

He was so close. He was so sure. He was so brave. And he was rubbing a pattern across her skin that was making her insides float in the air.

Guilt welled in her chest. "I didn't mean to hurt Brice. The burn was an accident."

"It was a splatter. Brice overreacted. He definitely wouldn't have survived muddied in a trench." Geoff clasped her hand to his heart as if it was his most prized possession. "Brice wouldn't have stayed one full day with me at the lodge. He barely lasted the night."

Was that a compliment? She tried to smile, but the weariness of the last hours weighed her down.

"I'm glad you're here." And she was glad. Geoff had become part of her life. A friend. A confidant. *A beau?* "Dr. Miller listened to you. I had forgotten what it's like to be frightened by the sound of your voice."

"I don't want you to be afraid of me ever again." Geoff's voice crackled with emotion. "I'm going to wrap you in blankets and spoil you for the next month."

"With flapjacks and fish?" She straightened to be as tall as Geoff.

"With whatever you want." He let go of her hand, got up, and pushed a wheelchair next to the bed.

She adjusted her sling. "We'll need to notify my mother before Ann's gossip reaches her ears."

"Not to worry. I'll send a message to Sophia. Better me waiting on you hand and foot than her." His strong arms steadied her as she sat in the wheelchair.

She reached up and wrapped a piece of his hair around his ear.

"You need a haircut."

"Seeing as you only have one hand, your left hand, it will have to wait. I'm definitely not giving Tubby shears."

"It can wait," she said. "Long hair makes you look younger."

"How young?"

"Young as me." Her cheekbones grew hot.

The wheelchair slowed, and started, and slowed again as Geoff pushed her out the door, and down the dock. He balanced himself with the chair and his walking stick. Stop and go. Stop and go. Fortunately, her nausea had subsided.

The May breeze enlivened her senses and dulled the lingering aroma of rubbing alcohol.

Geoff guided her toward the *Dorah*.

"You didn't come on the M*aiden*?" She remembered Tubby saying something about returning this morning.

"Nope. I came compliments of Todd Shipping. It was the least Brice could do after he saw how distraught I was when Tubby whisked you away from me."

Geoff may have come on the *Dorah* but the *Maiden* was slipped one dock over. Before she could ask about Tubby, she heard the captain holler. "Don't you dare put Jo on that imbecile's ship?" The stomp of Tubby's boots startled sea birds into flight. Tubby grasped Geoff's' coat. "I don't need Brice's charity. I brought Jo to Kat Wil on the *Maiden,* and I'll be taking her home on the *Maiden.*"

Geoff stepped forward to reason with Tubby.

The force of Tubby's pull on Geoff's coat caused Geoff to teeter on his wooden legs.

"Tubby, please," she shouted, "It's all right now."

"All right, is it? Look at yourself and tell me you're the picture of health." The captain seared Geoff with a hot hatred in his eyes. "What's her mother going to say when she sees those stitches?"

Geoff gripped Tubby's arms. "We're not going to Juneau. We're going to the lodge."

Tubby's head jerked toward Josephine. "Did that tree knock all the sense out of ya? How's a man with no legs going to take care of a dizzy woman with one arm?"

"We'll manage. Now both of you separate and

stop scaring me to death." Visions of Geoff plunging into the water seized her heart.

Tubby's thick finger pointed down the dock.

"Go," he shouted at Geoff. "I need to talk to Jo. Alone."

Geoff stood his ground. "You can't order me around. You're not her father."

"I'm the closest thing she's got to one, and if I don't see your backside heading toward that mine, I'll make sure you swim there."

She touched Geoff's back. "A few minutes won't hurt."

"Minutes." Geoff tapped his walking stick a few times before acquiescing to Tubby's order. He sauntered slower than normal.

Tubby paced in front of the wheelchair, his hands linked behind his back. "Why? Why go to the lodge? You can stay with my wife. She'll pamper you."

"My injuries weren't all Geoff's fault."

"Don't you let him off the hook. Whatever Brice started, he could have ended." Tubby knelt beside the chair. "Do you know what it was like carrying you in my arms? It was as if I carried my daughter. She died from a fever when she was a child." Wetness shone in the captain's eyes. "I can't handle a repeat of yesterday. I can't lose you. I care too much."

"You won't have to, Tubby. I promise." She laid her hand on top of his calloused fingers. "I want to go back to the lodge. I'm not a little girl anymore."

"That's another reason you should come home with me." Tubby glared down the dock at Geoff.

"Tubby, I want to go to the lodge." She jutted forward in earnest.

Tubby squinted and searched her face. His

expression did not waiver. Neither did hers.

"Would you go back to the lodge if Geoff wasn't there?" Tubby growled Geoff's name.

She picked at the cloth on her sling. "No, I wouldn't. He's the reason I'm going back. I've grown fond of him." There she had said it. Plain and true.

"I should have rescued you months ago when I had the chance. I should have asked more questions." Tubby removed his cap and wiped his brow.

She reached out and gave Tubby a one-armed hug. His white-gray hair was as soft as Wanda's stolen cotton balls. "You've rescued me once. You won't have to again. I promise."

Tubby stood and secured his cap. "If anything happens to you," his voice reverberated from ship to ship, "I get to strap Geoff to the prow of the *Maiden*. My own living figurehead."

Her forehead sparked with pain. "Could we strap Brice instead?"

30

Tubby carried her into the lodge as if she were made of heirloom china.

"Put her in my bed," Geoff said.

"The heck I will." Tubby knocked Geoff out of the way as he laid her on the living room couch. "Don't just stand there, Chambers. She'll need pillows, blankets, and something to drink. Hop to it, boy."

"When will you return this way?" Josephine asked as Geoff propped up her head and arm with more pillows than she remembered being at the lodge.

The captain grinned. "Sooner than you think. The front of my ship's looking barren and lonely." Tubby gave Geoff an over-protective-father glare. He headed for the door. The scent of apples and cinnamon trailed in his wake.

"Thank you, Tubby," Josephine said.

"Don't thank me. Geoff here is going to get you back shipshape." With a wink and a puff, he continued, "I'll visit soon with some baked goods from the wife. Wouldn't want you wasting away to nothing. Would we now, Chambers?"

"I'll take good care of her."

"You'd better," Tubby shot back. The front door closed with an extra loud thump.

"Are you comfortable?" Geoff balanced his weight on the edge of the couch.

"Yes, you've made a nice nest for me."

He didn't smile. The lines on his face deepened as if phantom pain tormented him.

"I'm going to make things right between us. I don't want anyone to take you away from me again."

The determination in his voice made her heartbeat surge. She snuggled into the pillows. Sleeplessness streamed into her veins. "I know you'll care for me," she assured him. If only he knew how much she cared for him.

"I do care, Jo." His fingers glided down her arm and cupped her hand. "I realized how much when you weren't here with me last night." A tic flared his jaw. He tilted his head backward. His eyes were moist, but no tears wetted his face. "I want you to stay at the lodge...with me."

The tenderness of his request made tears flood her eyes.

"Stay past June, past summer. I don't want to watch you dancing in another man's arms unless I know you'll end up in mine."

She slipped her hand from his and wiped the tears from her face.

He leaned closer inching higher on the couch. "I know it won't be easy—"

"I know what it's like." Her lips trembled as she smiled. "How can I leave you? You haven't bested me at rummy."

He came closer. His breath warmed her chin.

Closing her eyes, she waited for his kiss.

"Marry me."

Her eyes flew open. The tenderness in his voice

and the gleam in his eyes swept her away on an ocean breeze. Her spirit soared to the highest glacier.

She pressed her lips into his and waited for him to deepen their kiss. He didn't disappoint. Neither did she.

"Can I take that as a yes?"

There was no way she could refuse his proposal. Her face grew hot as her mouth curved into a dazzling smile of acceptance.

"Josephine Nimetz, for the first time in my life, I think I can read your face."

"You realize I come with a dog," she said, leaning forward to kiss him again.

"Is that all?" He laughed and removed a small velvet box from his pocket. "I thought you wanted me to type another manuscript."

"No, but have you ever thought about adding a wrap-around porch to the lodge?"

"Always thinking of me." He eased the tiny metal hinges open.

The lamplight played hide-and-seek with three diamonds set on a gold band. The large center stone, faceted to perfection, sparkled between a pair of smaller, equally impressive gems. Her chest pounded with excitement.

"My father gave this ring to my mother the day I was born."

"It's beautiful."

"Not as beautiful as you. Without you, I don't know if I would have gotten my life back." Tears glistened in Geoff's eyes. Not tears from split-open sores or phantom pains. These were tears she had not seen before, tears of love and happiness.

"Josephine Primrose Nimetz, will you have me as

your husband? I'd get down on one knee to ask, but I don't know how you'd get me up?"

She wanted to laugh, giggle, and sing all at the same time. "Yes, I will have you."

"When?" His arms draped loosely around her waist. "We can wait if you'd like? I can wait 'til you're nineteen, twenty, twenty-one? Whenever you're ready."

"I'm ready," she said, her body enjoying the touch of his embrace. "I've dreamed about being with you."

His eyes widened.

"You have? What did you dream?"

"That you came into my room," she paused, "and I let you slip into my bed to comfort me from a storm." His hands tightened around her waist.

"Did I have legs in your dream?"

"No legs, not even wooden ones. It was just you…and me, but I woke up before…"

His mouth found hers.

A few minutes later, he said, "I love you."

With her lips tingling, she nestled her limp body into the couch.

"How about November?" she asked. "After my nineteenth birthday and before Armistice Day. I want to show you off to the whole town."

"Your outstanding veteran?"

She liked that he remembered her praise. Even if it was during her outburst at the mine.

"And after Armistice Day," he said, "we'll take a trip wherever you want to go."

"But you told Brice traveling was too difficult."

"Traveling will be easy with you. You know how I…" He cocked his head to the side in thought of a word. "Work. You know how to assemble my parts."

A hint of a blush bathed his cheeks. "The difficult task is deciding what we're going to do until you're healthy enough to go back to Juneau? You can't match a hand of cards for rummy, writing will be a challenge, and sewing bridesmaid dresses is definitely out of the question."

"We'll play hide-the-ring from Tubby, and we'll pretend we're riding in a taxi. We'll need lots of Gregory-kiss practice for our honeymoon trip." She pulled his shocked, handsome face closer. "Won't our driver be surprised?"

~*~

A week after her return home from the mine's infirmary, Geoff led her to the couch. He fluffed a pillow for her arm to rest on. "I need to get my winning streak back."

She eased onto the cushions. "You're stuck as dealer."

"My penance." He shuffled and dealt, even looked away when she sorted her cards one-handed.

Shortly, she was within a few points of winning.

Holding the cards to her lips, she dared him to beat her.

Geoff leaned across the table. "Aren't you going to lay that card down?"

She giggled into her lucky spade.

"Josephine Primrose." His voice rose with a playful chastisement. "Lay down so I can see what you've got."

The door swung open.

Tubby held his pipe in hand; his gaze darted between the two card players.

"For Pete's sake. What's going on in here?"

"Gin Rummy." She and Geoff answered in unison.

"That all?" Tubby's bushy eyebrows arched. He belted out a laugh.

Geoff fanned his face with the cards.

She flashed the diamond ring hidden by her sling. "It's a good thing he knows I love you."

31

July 17, 1919
Wedding Reception of Ann and Marty Hill

"You don't think we're attracting too much attention away from Marty and Ann, do you?" Josephine took small steps as Geoff foxtrotted her across the dance floor. "It is their wedding day."

"If we are, it's Marty's fault for insinuating that you were attacked by a bear. And of course, there's the fairy tale you wrote about me—making me out to be the hero of Belleau Wood. Julia hasn't stopped apologizing for not understanding my circumstances. Not to mention, since I returned to Juneau, I can't walk down the street without someone thanking me for my service."

"I was honest about the struggles of your recovery but maybe a bit too generous with my praise. You're getting almost as much fan mail as me now."

"I think you're worrying about nothing," Geoff said, leading her in a calculated step. "Ann looks stunning in that creation of yours. People haven't taken their eyes off her or that dress. But I have to say, it's the bridesmaid in the orange gown that takes my breath away."

"It's peach. And it's amazing the designs you can buy when your employer is generous with your pay." She gazed up at Geoff and tightened her hold on his shoulder. She caressed the nape of his neck.

"You're leaning," he said with a satisfied grin.

"Would you like me to stop?"

"No." His mischievous eyes scanned the circle of men around the dance floor. "I like the hint of envy on their faces. I'll take envy over pity any day."

He guided her to the center of the dance floor oblivious to the rhythm of the music. "Are you coming for Sunday dinner? My father and Julia are anxious to discuss wedding plans with your mother."

"What a shame. Ann will be on her honeymoon," she kidded. "But I don't know about tomorrow. It might be a late night with all the festivities?"

"Can I tempt you with chocolate cake?"

"You don't need cake to entice me, but if you want to spoil me, how about chocolate cake with strawberry filling."

He pulled her closer. "Sounds good together."

"Always."

32

November 6, 1919
The Lodge

Mr. and Mrs. Geoff Chambers disembarked from the *Maiden* with as little help as possible. The minute Geoff's wooden legs and walking stick thumped the ground, Riley trotted down the gangway and raced toward the newly planked wrap-around porch. The dog's tail created a windstorm all its own.

"Oh, no. We should have left him in Juneau," Geoff said.

She gave her husband a quick kiss on the cheek. "Riley or Tubby?"

"Both. How hard is it to steer a ship?" He hugged her waist with his free arm. "Turn around and wave, would you? Tubby's glare is like two daggers being thrust into my back."

"You're imagining things. Tubby walked me down the aisle and gave me to you. He shed a tear during the nuptials."

"Come on, just one excited wave. I want the captain to warm to the idea of me being your husband."

Josephine turned on her heels and waved giddily

at Tubby, blowing him a kiss.

"Ah, relief." Geoff slouched briefly. "I love you, Jo."

Laughing, and with a glance to make sure Tubby was busy onboard the ship, she kissed Geoff. On. The. Lips. "I love you, too."

"You're making me weak in the knees."

"You don't have any knees."

"Exactly." Geoff grinned. "You weaken the invisible."

After they both had entered the lodge and latched the door, a scratching noise rattled the wood.

Should she ignore it?

"You might as well let our pet inside." Geoff's smile illuminated the lodge. "We won't be waiting on him later when he gets thirsty." He arched his eyebrows. "And look what needing a drink of water brought me."

She wrapped her arms around her husband and gave him an award-winning kiss. Not a Gregory kiss, but a Geoff kiss. An outstanding kiss for her outstanding veteran and her most outstanding companion.

Acknowledgements

This book would not have been possible without the help of so many people. My family has been my cheering section throughout my publishing journey. I am blessed to have their love and encouragement.

A big thank you goes to my editor, Fay Lamb, who corrects my mistakes and adds shine to my stories, and to Nicola Martinez for her continuing support of my writing and for her wise Christian leadership at Pelican Book Group.

My marvelous critique partner, Betsy Norman, makes me a better writer and she is a wonderful friend. The Barnes & Noble Brainstormers keep me focused on my stories and are a highlight of my week. Thank you, Jill Bevers, Denise Cychosz, Liz Czukas, Sandy Goldsworthy, Molly Maka, Karen Miller, Betsy Norman, Liz Steiner, Sandee Turriff, and Christine Welman.

I have a huge support system within the RWA community, SCBWI community, and the ACFW community. My fellow PBG authors encourage me every week. I am grateful. My church family in Wisconsin and countrywide has been a huge blessing to me as always.

And last, but definitely not least, to the Lord God Almighty, for giving me the gift of creativity and breath each day to write these stories. I am a cancer survivor, and not a day goes by that I don't praise the Lord for His healing. To God be the glory.

Author's Note

I hope you enjoyed Geoff and Josephine's story. The idea for their adventure came to me on an Alaskan cruise excursion. My family visited the Taku Lodge located outside of Juneau on the Taku River. While feasting on salmon, we were told that the lodge/camp was built in 1923 by Dr. Harry C. DeVighne and later sold to a wealthy Michigan family. The Smith family had a son who suffered from post-war health problems. The Smiths sent a nurse, Mary Joyce, to care for their son, and the two lived at the Taku Camp training Huskies. The veteran died, and Mary Joyce went on to mush Huskies and complete a thousand-mile sled trip. She was quite an exciting woman.

While I was eating lunch, and the story unfolded, I thought, a man and a woman alone in a lodge? I delved into what a WWI veteran might be suffering from and gave the veteran a spunky nurse from Juneau. My fictitious Gilbertsen lodge is based on the Taku Lodge, but I moved the lodge to Douglas Island where mining activity abounded. My lodge was built prior to 1918. In 1917, the Gastineau Channel broke through a wall of the Treadwell Mine and flooded it. You can visit that site on a cruise excursion, too. For my novel, the Kat Wil Mine is doing quite nicely in 1918 and beyond.

If you go to Juneau, you can also visit St. Nicholas Church. The church has been active since the 1890s. You can also visit historic sites about the darker side of mining, that being Wanda's profession.

Thank you for letting me indulge my "what ifs."

May the Lord bless you and keep you.

Barbara

You Can Help!

At Pelican Book Group it is our mission to entertain readers with fiction that uplifts the Gospel. It is our privilege to spend time with you awhile as you read our stories.

We believe you can help us to bring Christ into the lives of people across the globe. And you don't have to open your wallet or even leave your house!

Here are 3 simple things you can do to help us bring illuminating fiction™ to people everywhere.

1) If you enjoyed this book, write a positive review. Post it at online retailers and websites where readers gather. And share your review with us at reviews@pelicanbookgroup.com (this does give us permission to reprint your review in whole or in part.)

2) If you enjoyed this book, recommend it to a friend in person, at a book club or on social media.

3) If you have suggestions on how we can improve or expand our selection, let us know. We value your opinion. Use the contact form on our web site or e-mail us at customer@pelicanbookgroup.com

God Can Help!

Are you in need? The Almighty can do great things for you. Holy is His Name! He has mercy in every generation. He can lift up the lowly and accomplish all things. Reach out today.

Do not fear: I am with you; do not be anxious: I am your God. I will strengthen you, I will help you, I will uphold you with my victorious right hand.

~Isaiah 41:10 (NAB)

We pray daily, and we especially pray for everyone connected to Pelican Book Group—that includes you! If you have a specific need, we welcome the opportunity to pray for you. Share your needs or praise reports at http://pelink.us/pray4us

Free Book Offer

We're looking for booklovers like you to partner with us! Join our team of influencers today and periodically receive free eBooks and exclusive offers.

For more information
Visit http://pelicanbookgroup.com/booklovers

How About Free Audiobooks?

We're looking for audiobook lovers, too! Partner with us as an audiobook lover and periodically receive free audiobooks!

For more information
Visit
http://pelicanbookgroup.com/booklovers/freeaudio.html

or e-mail
booklovers@pelicanbookgroup.com